Raven

Magic

Renee Joiner

Raven Magic

©**2019 Renee Joiner**

www.oshunpublications.com

ISBN-13: 978-1-948834-93-3

Cover design by Michele Barrow-Belisle

Logo design by Monique Joiner Siedlak

Logo image by Pixabay.com

Magic of the Night

Raven Magic

To hear about future books by Renee Joiner, sign up for her new release newsletter, sign up here: https://mojosiedlak.com/reneejoiner-newsletter

Chapter One

Sitting crossed legged on the floor, Anja began to shuffle the deck as she concentrated on how to save her grandmother. In the middle of Anja's shuffling, one card shot out, hitting her on the forehead.

"Ow!" she cried, noticing it was the Magician.

Placing it back in the deck, Anja ignored it and took a deep breath. With her eyes closed began again, laying out three cards.

The first card she turned up was the world just looking at it she knew that it indicated to her that Anja would be traveling in the not-so-distant future but everything would work out she saw this as a message from the universe to have a more open mind and try to become more receptive and expand her awareness.

The next card she turned up was the Tower. She gasped. What kind of event would happen? What change was she about to make? What truth didn't she know? Anja knew something was going on and it had to do with the witches. But what it was, she didn't have a clue.

Holding the card in her hand, she wondered what it meant. Is it connected to Régine?

The last card of the spread. Once again the Magician appeared. Anja knew for sure the first time this card popped up wasn't an accident. Especially tonight.

It's the night before Summer's End or Samhain. A time-honored tradition followed by Witches, Wiccans, Ancient Druids and countless other modern pagans across the world. Celebrated as October transitions to November, it's where the veil is at its thinnest.

Anja's altar is covered with a dark purple cloth displaying moon and star accents of orange and gold. Glowing were three large pillar candles in burgundy, silver, and black.

Her incense of myrrh and frankincense wafted through the air.

The candle flickers, briefly showing Anja's features and coloring resembles that of some mixture of Latina; presumably South American given the prominent indigenous qualities. Standing 5' 7" tall, and leggy, Anja has a recognizable feeling about her as a water elemental.

On top were the few photographs of her mother as well as the amethyst necklace her mother wore in all the pictures. Just like before, Anja lit the candles in her memory, absently touching the stone.

Her grandmother, Régine, is all Anja has a family. Régine raised Anja after losing her mother in childbirth. To this day, Anja regrets being selfish, moody, not always connecting and at times, not grateful when all they had was each other. Now, facing the possibility that she may lose her, Anja was more afraid than she's ever been in her life.

Régine's aura gives hints of a noble queen. Her skin is dark; with almond-shaped eyes the color of the night sky. Her thick, wavy, black hair is shoulder-length and which Régine typically wears in an imaginative, eccentric style. With her slim build, her clothes are flattering. With features similar to Anja, most people thought they were mother and daughter.

Now, she lay in her bed, motionless, leaving Anja powerless.

Holding Régine's hand, "I will find out who did this to you," whispering to her. "To us. I will not lose you. I love you."

"Mom," Anja began, "thank you for bringing me into this world. There isn't a day that goes by that I don't miss you. I wish I could feel you near me. Especially now." Sitting quietly, she listened. Was this the year her mother would send her a message.

Casting a protection spell, Anja is more than surprised to see that it fails.

"My Goddess, this never happens."

Thinking quickly, Anja resorts to basic, every day, anyone-with-a-spell book-could-work magic. Still, it gave little results. Now she was scared. Her grandmother was under some paranormal attack that has not only her powers draining but her life-force as well.

Several minutes passed. Anja was so scared, she wanted to cry. The need to wallow in self-pity, but her grandmother needed her attention. As she walked towards the back room, she noticed a shaft of moonlight hitting her tarot cards.

A sign.

"Thank you, mother," Anja whispered, her hand automatically rubbing the amulet.

The cards did tell her what she didn't want to see. Anja wanted to overlook what it meant. There's only one person the magician would be. He possessed power over all elements.

Besides the fact that he was the one man she swore she would never see. But Anja had to save Régine no matter what the cost. No matter if she had to bargain with the Devil himself. Vincent Salazar.

Chapter Two

Vincent Salazar's doorbell rang. After just sitting on his sofa and opening a cold bottle of beer, he was getting ready for a match between his two favorite teams. Samhain was just another night to him, and tonight, he had a thousand dollars on tonight's game. Tonight was the one time of the year he just merely wanted to be alone.

"What the hell?" he thought, getting from his now warm spot.

As he walked to his door, his little toe hit the corner of the coffee table, which knocked his beer over the surface and onto his sofa.

"Fuck, Fuck fuck" Now he was really in a foul mood. He was going to take it out of whoever was on the other side of that door.

Almost at the door, the bell rang again.

"Damn it!" he fumed.

Vincent pulled the door forcefully shouting, his eyes flashing, "Yeah, what the hell do you want?"

Anja looked up at him with disbelief. "Is this the way you typically answer your door?" Anja asked.

Rubbing the back of his neck embarrassingly, "Anja, I'm sorry about that. I wasn't expecting any company tonight. You know, Samhain and all. Are you not enjoying the celebrations?"

Doing everything she could not look him directly in the eyes, she responded, "no, not tonight."

At 6' 3" tall, Vincent has an accustomed quality about him. He possesses a narrow face, a straight nose, full lips, large brown eyes, and tapered eyebrows. Some thought Vincent was a breathing work of art, his tanned skin so tantalizing to feel; each movement displaying his energy.

Vincent was unprepared to see Anja. Normally, he was calm, cool and collected. He was feeling like a school boy meeting his first crush. Which is exactly what Anja was.

Those mysterious, large light brown eyes she possessed. The pierced nose and a softly formed jaw. Anja now wore her short, curly, brown hair with a part in the center.

As always, her clothing is revealing and old, she has a persistent sweet smell about her. Vincent realized at that very moment, he still missed her.

"Look," Anja sniffed. "It was a huge mistake for me to come here."

Vincent quickly changed gears. Those eyes that could mesmerize him were red and puffy. He knew Anja was very upset.

"Is there something going on?" displaying genuine concern.

"Yeah, I wasn't expecting you to be home, but I had to try. Take a chance to see if you were home. I remembered you aren't big in the Sabbats and holidays."

Vincent tried to sound cavalier about it. "You know me. I was just about to watch a game. Besides, it's just another day. "

"I know," Anja confessed as she fidgeted with her amulet.

They didn't look at one another. The uneasiness grew, and the silence expanded.

"Look, Anja," he motioned for her to come inside, "with everything that's happened between the two of us, I know you didn't come here for small talk. What's going on?"

"Yeah, thanks. I didn't know who else to turn to about this." Unbuttoning her jacket, she sat on the couch putting distance between them and the spilled beer.

Anja looked at the bottle and then looked back up at him.

"Small accident," Vincent murmured thinking about his toe as he placed a pillow over the spot. "I'll get to it later."

"What's going on Anja? What's with the impromptu visit?"

"Have you heard about the draining of witches' powers? It started about a month ago."

"I have," he replied as he sat down on the sofa. With not much space left on the sofa, Vincent could see he sat closer than she preferred. "The way I understand it, is a paranormal attack?"

"Yes. That's what I believe it to be," Anja hesitated looking unsure.

"No one knows why it's happening or who is causing it?" Vincent questioned

Shaking her head, "Not yet," Anja acknowledged quietly.

"What does your grandmother think is going on? I'm sure you've asked her," he wondered.

"No, I haven't," Anja replied. Looking directly into Vincent's eyes, "Régine has been affected."

Vincent was momentarily speechless. "Not Régine. You're kidding me. You must be out of your mind!"

Taking a deep breath, Anja collected herself. "I'm doing everything I can not to. Régine needs me strong."

"What have you done to try to offset it?"

Throwing her hands up in the air, "I've done everything I can think of including the basics. Nothing is working. Nothing at all." Anja was close to being hysterical.

This surprised Vincent. He's never seen Anja lose her control. "You have every reason to be upset. Yell! Scream! Do you want to throw something?"

That last remark brought a small smile to her face.

"Look, the situation is more severe than has been let on. I know you have got to be freaking out."

"I am. There's one more thing Vincent."

"What?"

Anja struggled to share it with him withdrawing into herself once again. "My powers are also draining," she whispered.

That admission caused Vincent to hold her hands. They were colder than usual. Vincent knew this was not a good sign.

No wonder nothing is working. Anja, you must be frightened.

"Yes, I am. A few witches have died from this. Vincent," she whispered, "I don't want to be next or..."

"Régine," he whispered.

"Yes. Vincent. I can't lose her. I don't know what I would do if I did."

Anja had always been so self-conscious when she cried. No one, except for Régine has ever seen her cry. Really cry. Now she just fell way to the size of her anxiety.

"Come here Anja," Vincent whispered into her curly hair, "I think you need this more than you're willing to admit."

She sobbed into her hands and then into Vincent's embrace.

Vincent saw Anja shake with sorrow, tears streaming. Was part of him breaking too? Is this what happens when you love someone? Their comfort is a part of your own. As well as the problems.

Anja allowed herself to be pulled into his embrace. For the first time, in a long time, she thought about their time together. He still smelled so good. She could be herself without being judged. No matter how good it felt, she had to get back to Régine. She had already been gone too long.

Anja sniffed and pulled back. "I can't do this."

"Anja, it's okay."

"Vincent, I know this a lot to ask of you. You don't owe me anything. All I'm asking is can you come and look at her? See if there is anything you can do? Please?"

"Yes," he responded immediately without thinking about it. Vincent held her hands once more, "Anja; you shouldn't have felt afraid to ask me."

"With our history, I wasn't sure if I could or even should ask you."

"Anja, you know I always like Régine."

"I know. Régine is still fond of you."

They sat there in an awkward silence. Anja sniffed one more time.

"Okay, it's settled," he said as he reluctantly let go of her hands. "I'll be ready in a few, and we'll head out. I'm sure between the two of us; we can figure this out."

"All right. And Vincent?"

"Yeah?"

"Thanks for your help. This means a lot to me."

"I know what Régine means to you. I would be amiss if I didn't at least try to help."

Anja watched Vincent go into his bedroom. A weight now lifted from her shoulders. She knew Vincent would help her grandmother and then she would figure out what to do about her waning powers.

Vincent softly closed the door to his bedroom, flicking on the light switch. He started reminiscing both the good and the pain at losing her. It was great while it lasted. Great to be loved, the smile in Anja's eyes, the warmth of her cheek next to his. Her soft hand as she would rub his day old stubble. One of the reasons he now shaved less often.

It was great to be loved by Anja, but when it came to giving her more, his times as a teen with no home moved to the surface. When she left, he felt isolated and alone. No one to care for him, no one to laugh with him. His friends were now the next highest bidder.

While waiting for him to come back, Anja looked around Vincent's apartment. She noticed how well he must be doing. He's still the same Vincent she remembers with his tailored, sporty clothes He now has a sizeable runic tattoo over his entire right arm and small silver hoops in both ears. It seems like their breakup was probably the best thing that ever happened to him.

Walking around, she touched some of his souvenirs and keepsakes. Spying a picture of him with a young woman caused her a momentary lapse of jealousy.

"Why should I be jealous? I'm the one that broke it off with him, not the other way around. Besides I'm glad to see that he has moved on."

Instead of getting lost in her thoughts and memories, she decided to keep her hands busy she went ahead and clean up the mess that he had made earlier instead of touching his mementos.

Anja took the pillow and empty beer bottle into the kitchen. Spotting the dish towels, dampened one to clean the area on the sofa and floor and just as quickly, dried. She completed the task before Vincent made it back.

"I meant to ask," Vincent asked, startling her, "how did you get here? I know you were never fond of driving. I seem to recall you always thought I drove too fast."

"I took a bus. Taxi service is still on strike."

"You really did need to send me. What would you have done if I wasn't home?"

"Since you were, I guess we'll never know."

"I guess we won't," he replied as he opened the front door for her placing his hand at the small of her back to lead her out. The surge of electricity ran through them both.

Chapter Three

Anja stared straight ahead, only half-aware of a world outside the claustrophobic comfort of the truck. It was Vincent's hands stroking the wheel, the almost soundless changing of the gears, the closeness of him, which keep her attention. Vincent always drove fast, this evening was no exception.

She knew he drove fast. Too fast for her taste. In this instance, she wasn't bothered by it. She had to get back home as quickly as she could. Learning to drive was the one thing she never got around to since everything she needed was in walking distance.

Ten minutes later, they were pulling up into the front yard of Régine's small home. Most of the homes in the rural were small, and hers was no different. The reflective balls showed the way to the front door as they passed the big stone covered with a blanket of moss.

"I hope she's okay," Anja answered as they walked up the sidewalk.

"Who is she with?" Vincent asked her.

"Our neighbor, Maria. She lives down the road. I told her I would be back as soon as I could."

Unlocking the front door, "Maria! We're back."

"Getting some water," Maria called from the kitchen.

With observant, large hazel eyes, a small nose, and a softly shaped jaw, Maria is entirely bald. Always wearing a headband and with matching sneakers, today's color is hot pink. Maria, as a tall and stout woman with dark skin, came equipped with a quick temper. If she didn't like you, she had no problem letting you know.

Anja and Vincent walked to Régine's bedroom. With Maria was right behind them, Vincent could literally feel her eyes boring into the back of his skull.

"Is there any change Maria?" Anja asked looking at her grandmother.

"No Anja," Maria swallowed hard, demanding her eyes to remain dry. "Your grandmother is just motionless. You have to look very closely to see that she is still breathing."

"Maria, this is Vincent. I've asked him to look at Régine, and maybe we can figure out how to slow this down, if not stop it altogether."

Maria crossed her arms as she eyed Vincent with his tailored look.

"You are not afraid what has happened to them will not occur to you?" he asked her.

Vincent could almost hear the mocking tone in her voice. "I am not. Aren't you?"

Raising his hand towards Maria, he could sense she was not a witch.

"Nope, Mr. Magic Man," she vocalized as she wagged her finger in front of Vincent. "I'm human. With no powers at all. Therefore, not in danger."

"Well, not this type of magical danger."

"Maria is a nurse," Anja sounded, cutting in, "and the perfect person to watch Régine while I went out."

"Yeah, your number doesn't work. You might want to check that out."

"Maria!" Anja exclaimed. She was both shocked and embarrassed by her friend's crassness.

"What? It's true," Maria clucked looking at Vincent accusingly. "You wouldn't have to go out. You're suffering from the same thing."

"If I had known Anja would have needed my number or wanted to get in contact with me, she would have had my new phone number."

Anja pulled her into a grateful hug. "Maria, we didn't part on good terms. That's how serious this is if I desperately need his help. Please be nice."

"Well, if you say so." In a huff, "I'll be in the living room," looking at Vincent, "just in case you need me."

"I say so. Thanks, Maria"

"Okay," Vincent began now exasperated, "let me give Régine a scan. I need to know what I'm working with."

Vincent pulled two shungite stones from his pocket. Placing one on top of Régine's head, he held the other in his hand, moving it down the length of her prone body and went back up. Anja watched fascinated as they seem to glow in synchronization. Anja always had loved watching him. His ease and grace of movement fluid motion were mesmerizing.

"Hmm," Vincent expressed absently.

Anja could see he was perplexed, but she wanted answers. She was too impatient to wait quietly.

"What, do you see? What's the verdict?" Fear crossed her face.

Vincent pondered for a moment.

"I have never felt this type of attack before. I'd say whoever did this, it's personal for them."

"Personal? Why? Régine never hurt anyone. Everyone loves her."

"All I know is what I'm reading. It's not good."

"My powers are waning, am I under the same attack?"

"Maybe," he replied. "Look, hold this stone to your forehead and let me perform the same scan on you."

Doing as he asked, Anja stood there as Vincent moved the stone down and up her body.

Anja allowed her eyes to follow him. As they began to move up, their eyes locked for a brief moment.

"Well? How bad is it?" Anja asked, breaking the tension.

"You both are under the same attack — no doubt from the same person."

"But why is Régine in a coma?"

"I believe it's affecting Régine quicker than you because of her age. Also, she's more powerful than the other witches that have passed on. Her coma is a way of her body slowing down the process. It's a form of protection. However, if we don't find a way to stop this, she loses this fight."

"Lose? You mean die?"

"Yes, I'm afraid I am."

"How long?"

"How long?"

"Yes! How long before she cannot hold on any longer?" Anja was almost shrieking, giving in to her anger and pain.

"Right now, maybe five days. I don't believe Régine will last a week."

"Oh, my Goddess," she said touching her necklace as her voice became shaky.

Vincent grasped Anja's shoulders. "Look, I am not going to let you give up. There is a way we can cure her."

"There's a way?" she sniffed.

"I wasn't going to mention it, because how dangerous it is but it seems you may not have any other choice."

"Vincent, I'm at the point of last resorts. What is it?"

"The sacred waters from the Well of Rites."

"Really?"

"With the sacred waters from the Well of Rites, you can save her."

"Everyone who has ever attempted that journey has either been badly injured or died."

"Not everyone," Vincent noted.

"Has anyone ever made it there and back?"

"I have."

"Really? I never knew." Anja had a look of disbelief. "You have gone to the Well of Rites and didn't get hurt?"

"Yes, I believe it's why I'm not being affected. It's something I don't talk about and still prefer not to."

Noticing the dark expression come across his face, she let the subject drop, for now.

"The only thing is the Elemental witch that guards the well. She's going to want payment."

"I'll give her anything. Sell everything if it means saving Régine."

"It's not money she wants. It never is. You have to be willing to sacrifice something you are unwilling to part with — the most important thing to you."

"I don't have anything."

"There's nothing at all? Everyone has something."

"No, I don't."

Vincent stared at her neck. It was at that point she absently touched her mother's magic amulet. A beautiful aquamarine stone her mother always wore.

"No. I cannot give up my mother's amulet. It's all I have left of her along with a few vague memories."

"That's why she demands a sacrifice. If that's the one thing you treasure most, you must be willing to part with it."

Anja ran her fingers over the stone. "I'll have to find something else."

"No, the witch can see into your soul. She will know what your true sacrifice is and what is not."

Looking her directly in the eyes, Vincent spoke to her in a way that gave her chills.

"You cannot fool her. Believe me."

"Vincent, Régine made me swear never to lose this. She made me swear."

"I understand that Anja, but..."

"No buts. It was the most important thing my mother had next to me. I can't just give it away. I can't."

"Then there is nothing more I can do here." Vincent actually sounded defeated. "I'm sorry Anja. I'll see myself out."

As Vincent headed to the front door, he stopped to speak to Maria.

"Look, Maria, I sense you don't like me."

Folding her arms across her chest, "this is true."

"But Anja is going to need someone to lean on."

"So you cannot help her or Ms. Régine?"

"I can, but Anja has to choose between of the most important people in her life. She may need you here when she comes to a decision." Pulling a card out of his pocket, "here's my number. Give it to her when she's has made her decision."

"Humph, I guess you're not all that bad Mr. Magic Man."

Flashing a smile at her that made her blush, "please, call me Vincent."

Anja could hear Vincent's truck as he drove away. What was she going to do?

In Régine's room, there were lots of mementos some from trips such as Bali, the Taj Mahal, times when she went skiing in the Alps. There were also pictures when she traveled with Anja's mother, Emma. Anja could see her mother was happy growing up. There was a sparkle in her eyes.

One of Anja's yearly birthdays present was to pick one of the photos to keep in her own room. Last year, it was a picture of her mother blowing out a candle on her fifth birthday. Anja hopes that this year she would be able to pick one with her mother and grandmother together.

"Régine, I wish you could tell me how to help you. I can't choose between you and my mother."

Maria entered the room. Nodding towards the front door, "He says you have to make a decision."

"Yes Maria," she sniffed.

"What does your heart tell you?" Maria asked her in a soft voice.

"I have to choose. But what if I make the wrong choice?"

"All I can say is if you make a choice, you must stand behind it. Don't second guess yourself."

Anja didn't even have to think about it. "Maria, I have to save Régine."

Handing Anja the card, "He knew you would need this. Call him."

Feeling like she didn't have any other choice, Anja called Vincent.

"You're really doing the right thing, Anja," Vincent assured her once he answered his phone.

"I know," she spoke solemnly.

"The Well of Rites will save Regina."

"Your right, if that's what it will take, but to give up my mother's amulet, I don't know. I can't lose her though."

"It is a dangerous trip, Anja," Vincent reminded her. "That's why I'm going with you."

"I know this is something neither of us would really want," Anja said, hinting at their past relationship.

"Anja I still care about you," Vincent revealed. "No matter how I tried to forget you."

"I'm sorry Vincent, this something I don't want to think about right now my main concern right now is Régine. That's it."

Vincent could hear she was getting upset. He let her continue before saying anything.

"I don't have time for how you feel or how I feel. I would have preferred not to call you in the first place."

Taking a deep breath, he continued, "You always let your pride stand in your way."

"Sometimes my pride is all I have left. This is why I could never abide by all your lies."

"I never lied to you about how I feel never, and you know that."

"Hiding things, the omission, it's same as lying and you know I need the truth at all times I can't live my life with uncertainty."

"Enough!" he spoke firmly to her. "We'll talk about this another time. Right now, go ahead and get yourself a good night's sleep. I will be there early. I'll be there about eight? We will need to be on the road early."

"Okay. And Vincent?"

"Yeah."

"I'm sorry I attacked you," she said sheepishly, now feeling foolish.

"Don't worry about it. You're just worried about Régine."

Anja hung up the phone and thought about what she just committed herself to. She would go to a place most people never returned from to help her grandmother. It was a risk, she may not come back. Her grandmother, Régine was well worth it. Even if she would be spending her time with the Devil himself.

Chapter Four

"Are you ready?" Vincent asked when he returned in the morning. Surveying clothes strewn over her couch, he didn't think so.

"Just about," she expressed over her shoulder. "Maria is getting herself settled in."

"She'll stay here with Régine?"

"Of course. There's no one else I'd trust."

"That's an excellent idea. I've brought a few extra stones with me. I want to reinforce the protection spell I placed on her last night and put one on Maria if she allows me."

"I don't think Maria will mind. I don't know what you said to her, but she is singing a different tune about you."

"Well, once you get to know me."

"Remember, I do know you. So you can stop wasting your charms on me."

"I'm just trying to keep this as less awkward as possible."

"Yeah, well," motioning toward Régine's room, "might as well reinforce the protection now. The sooner we get on the road, the sooner Régine can be healed."

As Vincent walked to back, Anja watched his body tense and then slowly release. Did she imagine things, or was Vincent nervous? If so, then what?

Maria greeted him with a smile.

"It looks like my day is getting better," he indicated to her, returning her smile.

"I don't know what it is. I feel everything is going to get better. Perhaps it's something Ms. Régine is feeling."

"Even in this state, she's aware of what's going on. I know Anja appreciates you watching over her grandmother while we retrieve a cure for her. But I would also like to thank you. Régine is the most important woman in her life. It's a terrible thing to be adrift with nothing or no one to anchor you."

"It sounds like you're speaking from experience."

"Perhaps. Look, before we go, I'm going to reinforce my spell from last night. I am also going to enclose you within it just in case. Do I have your permission?"

"Yes, you do," Maria said, sitting down, then closing her eyes.

Citing the incantation and placing crystals about, the energy began to rise. Once the blue sphere began to settle down, Vincent handed Maria a black obsidian crystal.

"It's beautiful," she said in awe, holding it in her hand. She could almost feel the smoothness seeping inside her soul. It warmed her body.

"Black obsidian is a powerful crystal for witches, elementals, shamans, and so on. Anything that involves the breaking of curses, hexes, spirit attachments, returning of energy to its sender. So many seek out this one stone it's become difficult to find."

"Wow!" Maria still amazed. "I wouldn't have known that something so beautiful had so much power."

"See," he said patting her hand. "There's a lot out there many don't know. Keep it with you at all times."

Sliding it into her pocket, "I will."

Placing another under Régine's pillow, "the two of you will be safe until we return," Vincent informed her.

"I do believe that."

"You know what, I also do," Anja said as she stood in the doorway. "I'm ready to go."

"Okay, I'll get you things in the truck."

Anja hugged Maria. "Thanks again for staying with Régine."

"You know there is no reason to thank me. Just go and come back soon."

"I will."

Kissing Régine on her forehead, Anja whispered. "Hold on. I know you can hold on. I love you so much."

Vincent was standing by the door. She saw that her bag was no longer on the floor. He probably already placed in the truck.

Anja knew the last leg of the journey would be done on foot, so broken in boots was going to be necessary. Grabbing an old pair out of her closet, she checked on Régine once more, and they were on their way.

Starting the truck, Vincent mentioned to her, "Before we head out on the road, we are going to need a few more items. I also think I should hold on to your mother's amulet. We do not want anything to happen to it."

"I don't think so," answering with a quickness. "It's been safe with me all this time. I should continue to keep it with me."

"But I still have my powers," he reminded her. "I just want to make sure you and it get to the well."

"Just why wouldn't it?" she questioned him. "I'll hold onto it."

Anja looked at him as he shrugged his shoulders and began collecting items for their trip. She wanted to trust him, but something inside was holding her back.

"It looks like we're in store for a bit of rain," Vincent said as the morning slowly darkened.

"I was hoping that we would be long gone before it hit," Anja absently said thinking how speed and rain do not mix.

"It's fine. I will get us safely to the foot of the mountains perhaps just after nightfall."

The rain hammered on the truck. It was a booming rhythmic sound on the metal hood as they drove southeast to the mountain of Syr.

Anja gazed blankly out the window. The darkening skies outside made the truck feel like a tightly enclosed space adding to the mounting anxiety burning deep in her stomach.

Reaching over to adjust the vent on her side after turning the heat on, Vincent wanted her to talk to him. Anja didn't feel much like talking.

"This will work out, Anja. We will retrieve the water. Everything will be fine," he said to her with a smile. There was an air of genuine excitement in his voice.

She nodded. All Anja could think about was Régine and what would happen if it didn't work.

The rain had stopped by the time they reached Tarvana. It was well past seven. For the first time, Anja realized that she was more than hungry. She was famished.

Anja let out a breath, silently. She was attempting to release some of the anxiety inside her. Assuring herself it would all be fine, Anja glanced over at Vincent. He noticed and grinned at her. Anja gave him a tight-lipped forced smile in return. She turned her attention back to the clouds beyond the truck window slowly moving away.

The motel Vincent pulled up to can only be described as non-descript. There were few cars in the parking lot, but that was mainly due to the caution signs put up to pardon the appearance as they renovate .

"Let's get our rooms and get something to eat."

"Yes, please. I'm starving." Anja said, placing her hand on her belly.

"I know. I heard your stomach growl more than once in the past couple of hours."

Blushing, she replied, "Well I haven't had much of appetite over the past couple of days."

They each grabbed their bags. The beep of the alarm system was loud in the quiet night.

The motel entryway's odor reminded Vincent of his former group home. Anja ignored it. The floor carpeting is a decade too old and with a traditional fashioned design of large blossoms disrupted by frayed and threadbare spots. The big windows should provide a lot of light, yet the heavy drapes and city grime on the panes give it a dull appearance to the point of desperation.

The clerk stood short with tan skin. He watched them coming in as he removed the black wired glasses framed his dull blue eyes. Running his fingers through his short, kinky, brown hair, he acknowledges Anja and Vincent.

Even with his scruffy, tacky form-fitting clothes, he has a warm friendliness feeling about him. Anja was getting a "favorite Uncle" vibe.

"Evening folks. Are you looking for a room with a queen or king sized bed?"

Clearing his throat, Vincent looked at Anja, She quickly gave him a look before he said, "Do have two rooms with full sized beds? Preferably adjacent?"

Checking the registry, the clerk shook his head.

"Sorry folks, the best I can do would be two adjoining singles."

"Fine, it'll do," Anja said, moving her bag to her other shoulder.

Her room was sparse, but she didn't care. The room included a small bed, neatly made, a dresser, without a mirror and a couch.

The couch had unquestionably seen better days. The battered decorative pattern was worn thin in areas but not really to the point of splitting. The blue-gray piping material encompassing the seats had the beginnings of fraying. It held the look and smell of dampness in the middle of one cushion.

A large housefly was droning furiously up and down trying to get out.

Deciding to leave her rucksack on the bed instead, Anja opened the door to shoo the fly out. She noticed a small diner next door. What she wanted right now was food, then sleep.

Turning on the light switch of the bathroom, she located a washcloth.

"Why am I even bothering to freshen up?" she said to herself. "This is just a quick meal with an acquaintance who has offered me their assistance. Nothing more, nothing less. We will go our separate ways once this is over."

The knock began softly first. Trying to act as if she wasn't anxious, Anja didn't open the door until he knocked the second time.

"Sorry about that."

"Don't worry about it," Vincent said just a nonchalantly. "We need a good dinner after that drive."

"Yes. I hope the cafe serves burgers and fries. Really can go for some fries."

"Same here."

Shutting off the room light and locking the door, they walked past the motel's office and into the cafe.

Chapter Five

The dark stranger, hidden in the shadows, watched Vincent and Anja walk towards the small diner. This was the time.

Walking into the motel's office, the stranger asked the clerk for a room. Luck would have it; the room was right across from Anja's room.

Clearing his voice, the clerk asked, "How long are you planning on staying?"

"Not long. Just long enough to complete what I need to get done."

Taking a second glance, "You look familiar. Have you been here before?"

"No, you haven't this is my first time here." Looking around, "How late is the diner open?"

The clerk looked at the stranger again possibly searching for a vague memory. "You know, I have a knack with faces. Sure you haven't been here before?"

"I just said I haven't," now getting impatient. "Can you tell me about the diner? It's hours?"

"Oh yeah, basically open 24/7. Unless Cookie can't make it in. That's the cook's name. Cookie." The clerk slapped the register's counter and laughed. "We thought it was pretty funny when she started working here."

Blowing out a breath, "That's good to know."

"Do you have any luggage for your room?"

"Nope. Just my backpack and that's enough. Can I just get my key?"

"Sure, sure. No problem. People say I like to talk a lot. I think it's one thing that most people seem to lack."

"I'm kind of in a rush here."

But the clerk just rambled on.

"You know the art of conversation?"

"My key... please!"

"Oh yeah. Here you go," turning the ledger around.

A simple thanks was mumbled.

"Go ahead sign here and here is your key. Enjoy your stay."

The dark stranger walked to room three. Flipping on the light the room was quickly surveyed.

"Now I just have to get what I come for."

Walking into the diner, Vincent and Anja saw that it wasn't quite full. It wasn't quite empty either. There looked to be a few of the current motel residents were here having a late dinner.

The diner had square tables for couples, larger rectangle one for a larger group. With glass tops, the menus were underneath. Safe from spills and that one child who enjoys tearing everything up. The ceiling fans above turned slowly. The daily special on a chalkboard at the entrance was smeared. Light classical rock played from the jukebox.

Vincent laughed when he saw the old-time jukebox standing in the corner.

"Wow haven't seen one of these in a very long time."

"I know what you mean. I wonder how far back the music goes," Anja responded.

"Good evening you two," the waitress in her mid-thirties greeted them. "We're not fancy here so go ahead find you a place to sit. I will be right there with you to get your order."

"Thank you very much," Vincent said.

Picking a table away from the kitchen, Anja allowed herself to take a deep breath. Looking at the menu, she saw they served hamburgers and fries. Things were looking up.

"I see that smile," Vincent said as they placed their order.

"Things can't be that bad when fries are involved," Anja said laughing.

They had a few minutes before their order would arrive, so Anja knew it was time to talk things through.

"I need to ask you a question, Vincent."

He knew it was coming sooner or later. Steeling himself, "go ahead."

"So, the Well of Rites located in a cavern within the mountain of Syr."

"True."

"A place few have survived unscathed. Most have not returned."

Vincent tapped on the table, "That isn't entirely true."

"No," leaning in towards him, "you said you'd been there."

"Yes I have, and as you can see, I did return."

"Can I ask you what your heart desire was?"

Did he just squirm in his chair?

"What was so important you would risk everything?" Anja wondered.

"Since I am going back, I guess I can tell you." Vincent knew there's no going back now, "I wanted to be powerful. To have unlimited power."

"Unlimited power?" Anja was amazed. "Really? That was your heart desire?"

"Anja, there is so much about me; you don't know." Clasping his hands behind his head, "I never told you everything about my life."

Avoiding his eyes, "That was one of our biggest problems," she responded quickly.

"Well, it's the reason why my power hasn't diminished as the witches and elementals have. How I was able to shore up enough energy for your grandmother. Since she is unconscious, she isn't expending any real power. The spell will help maintain her."

"But it wouldn't work on me?" Anja asked. "You couldn't keep me from losing my powers?"

"Sadly, no. Unless you were in a similar state, right now I'm only preventing her from slipping any further. It would take much more to do the same for you."

"So the well is not only Régine's best option, it's mine too?"

"Yes," Vincent explained to her. "The water will bring her out of her coma and keep you from losing your power altogether." Shrugging his shoulders, "After that, you will no longer have a fear of losing your powers."

"I have so many more questions. When did you go?"

"Well," Vincent said, leaning back in his chair, knowing he just dodged a bullet, "here comes our waitress."

"Saved by the fries." Anja bit into the first fry, "Mm, perfection."

* * *

The dark figure watched them through the windows. They looked like the perfect couple. Laughing and enjoying their meal. They also had something essential, and it was time to relieve them of it.

"Enjoy yourselves now. Tomorrow is another day."

Remaining unseen, the lock to Anja's room was easy to pick.

The plan was to leave the room intact, but desperation began to creep in after coming up empty.

"Where is it?"

The dark figured wanted to scream. Wanted to tear the room apart.

"There's no way I'm leaving empty-handed. I can't."

Taking a deep breath, the dark figure devised another plan.

* * *

Swirling her last fries in the ketchup, Anja quickly popped it into her mouth. "I don't know the last time I enjoyed a meal so."

"Maybe it was the company," Vincent said as Anja licked the ketchup off her finger.

"Maybe."

Placing some cash on the table, "why don't you order dessert? One for me also."

"Where are you going?" she asked

"I need to get something out of the truck. I'll be right back."

As Vincent left the cafe, she signaled the waitress and asked for the check. Even the waitress asked Anja if she wanted dessert, she shook her head.

As she walked out of the cafe, there was no sign of Vincent at his truck. A few minutes later, she saw him coming from the direction of their room.

"I thought you were going to your truck."

"I was. I saw someone who looked like they were checking the vehicle doors. I lost them running through the small alley."

"Good thing you locked your door."

"Of course, I did."

"If someone really wanted to get in, locks wouldn't stop them."

"I guess you're right."

"Well, to be on the safe side, make double sure you've locked your door."

They walked the rest of the way back to the rooms in silence. There were so many thoughts going through Anja's head at that moment, and she didn't feel like talking.

"I forgot to ask you," Vincent started, "what happened to our dessert?"

"Another time. I want to reach the cavern as soon as we can tomorrow."

"Okay," as they stopped at her door. "Good night then."

"Good night Vincent."

Vincent stared at the closed door for a full minute before he moved on to his room next door.

Once in his room, he took a deep breath sighing, "Idiot." Vincent chastised himself. He already knew how she felt about secrets .

The long drive and the heavy meal made Anja extremely tired. It was a good thing too. Tomorrow she and Vincent would make the twenty-mile hike up the mountain. The only way up there was to walk it. She took a quick shower to save time in the morning. Putting on her sleep shirt, she pulled her hair up in a puff and went to bed.

Lying there, Anja looked up at the ceiling attempting to sort out her thoughts and feelings from the past couple of days. Her only pressing question was will she finish this quest and return to Régine in time?

"But what about Vincent?" her inner voice whispered.

"We aren't together and for a good reason. Without trust, there's nothing."

"But, he did offer to help," that nagging voice added.

Turning to her side as she started to drift to sleep, her last thought was, "I can't just wait for the other shoe to drop."

Vincent lay on his bed with his arms behind his head. He had to admit, and he did miss Anja. She could always make him laugh.

"She's still as stubborn as ever," he said to himself with a slight chuckle.

"Starting over with Anja wouldn't be a bad idea. As long as she thought it was hers."

Whoa! Where did that come from? Vincent was enjoying his life the way it was right now. Why complicate it?

The figure moved stealthily in Anja's room. It took a long time until the rhythmic breathing of sleep could be heard. Pulling

Anja's rucksack slowly on the floor, the contents were searched meticulously.

Hearing Anja cough in her sleep, the figure froze. Not moving until once again, Anja was sound asleep. Taking the rucksack in hand, the figure headed towards the door with it.

"Who's there?" Anja cried out as she sat upright in her bed.

As she tried to turn one of bedside light on, a spark hit it and it wouldn't come on.

"Oh no, you don't," Anja yelled casting a lightening water spell.

With her powers so weak, it doesn't give her enough illumination to see who it is.

While dropping Anja's rucksack to the floor, the figure snatched the door open and ran into the night.

Realizing she only had one piece of clothes on; she didn't run after the stranger.

Anja saw the light on in Vincent's room. Not allowing her shirt to inch up anymore, she knocked. When he didn't answer, she tried again.

At that moment, coming around the corner, was Vincent.

"Anja, what are you doing up this time of night?"

"I could ask you the same thing. I thought you turned in for the night."

"I couldn't sleep so I went for a run."

Was that really sweat from going from a run or just running from her room?

"Really? The same time someone happens to break into my room?"

"It just so happens that I run when I can't sleep," Vincent informed her.

Anja eyed him, "You couldn't sleep? Why is that?"

Changing the subject quickly, Vincent pointed out to her "It's not important. Look, let's go back into your room. You shouldn't be out here half dressed."

Seeing a few curtains move by the other guests, Anja knew he was right.

Once Anja saw the light was unplugged, she plugged it back. Her room seemed to be brighter than before. Perhaps from her own spell.

"You saw someone in your room?" Vincent asked walking in behind her.

"I did," Anja explained. "It was dark, and I couldn't get my illumination spell bright enough."

"The light?" Vincent was puzzled.

"Whoever it was, is a witch. The cord pulled itself right out of the wall."

"Was it a man or a woman?"

"I don't know. Without any light to see by, it could have been anyone, even..."

"Me?"

"Sorry."

Exasperated, Vincent threw his hands in the air.

"Answer one thing. Why would I break into your room? What would I search for?"

She reached into her shirt. "Perhaps they were looking for my mother's amulet.

Since it's the only thing I have to give to the elemental witch, I keep it with me at all times."

"I see. Since I asked to keep it for safe keeping, you think that I would take it," said Vincent angrily as he took a step back from her.

"I'm sorry, Vincent. It's just things don't add up."

"Still, I am trying to help you. Help Régine. I don't know what more I can do."

All Anja could do was look at him. She could see that her accusation hurt Vincent, but in the back of her mind, it could all be just a trick.

"Look, I'm going back to my room. I say we head out at morning light. It's a long way there and a long way back."

"Okay," Anja was exhausted at this point.

The moment the door closed behind him, Anja knew she had never felt so alone. She crossed the room to the window and watched him stand there before moving on to his room.

Maybe he wants to help. Once more, Anja checked her bag; she was confident everything was there. Starting to feel the adrenaline ebb, Anja went back to bed. But not before pushing the room's small desk in front of the door.

"I want to see you come in this room without me knowing," talking to the intruder who was no longer there.

Anja thought about turning the light off but then decided to leave the bedside lamp on. Just in case.

* * *

Entering his room, Victor knew something was amiss. He could feel the slight remnant of magic that wasn't there earlier. There was only one thing inside someone would want to take, if they knew he had it. Looking under the dresser, Vincent saw it was gone. How was he going to explain this to Anja? She already didn't trust him, and if she knew a map existed, a map that was now gone, she would probably think that he put all this in motion to keep her from making the journey on her own.

"I'm just going to have to come clean with her," thinking to himself. That is the first thing Vincent planned on doing in the morning.

One thing for sure, someone knows why they are here and where they are going. Vincent could understand taking the map, but why the pendant? Unless they wanted to stop Anja altogether. But who would do such a thing?

Vincent lay down on the bed and started to drift off. The last image he was Anja dressed in just a large shirt.

"Don't go there," he chided himself as he placed his hand on his bulge and finally fell asleep.

* * *

The dark figured held one of the two objects that were desperately needed.

Slowly opening the map, the trail would seem to be more accessible than expected.

"I've got to find a way to relieve her of that amulet. If I don't, then all of this will have been for nothing."

Rolling the map back up, the dark figured returned to room three to try and get some rest.

"I will be close behind them when they leave in the morning."

Chapter Six

Vincent knocked on Anja's room door at first light. She thought she would be getting more sleep. Apparently, Vincent had other plans.

"Good morning," she said still yawning when she opened the door.

"Morning, Anja," Vincent said, as he looked to see if any other motel residents were being disturbed. "Sorry for the early wake-up call. I thought we should get moving as early as possible."

Even though she was half awake, by his demeanor, she could tell he was agitated about something.

"What's going on, Vincent?" she asked as she ushered him into her room.

Walking inside, Vincent sat down on the one chair in the room. "Apparently, you were not the only one to have someone break into your room last night."

"What do you mean?" Anja questioned. "Someone broke into your room?"

"Yes," he hesitated, dreading the need to tell her the rest.

"When?" Anja replied with a focused gaze.

"It had to be after leaving your room," he said making minimal eye contact. "Whoever it was last night came into mine."

"How could that be?"

"Remember," he started, "I didn't go back to my room right away."

Anja nodded, replying, "I know. Someone just ran from my room."

"Yes, and even though I placed a ward in my room," he admitted, "It was circumvented."

"Damn it! What could you have that someone would want? It had to be another witch."

"Yes. Not only that, it's what was taken."

"Which is what?" her eyes narrowing at his admission of hiding something else from her. Anja waited for whatever he didn't want to tell her.

"A map to the well," he finally conceded.

"A map?" Anja threw her hands up in the air "Do you mean to tell me you had a map? This entire time?"

"Yes, but Anja, let me explain," he pleaded before she was furious.

"Explain what?" Anja frowned as she pointed at him. "The fact I didn't need you to come with me. I could have done this alone."

"Just listen. You should know there is no way I would have allowed you to perform this trip on your own." Vincent stood directly in front of her to be sure he made the point, and Anja was not happy about it.

"You are a woman alone. Traipsing around alone is not only stupid, but it's suicidal. Régine would murder me if anything happened to you and I could have prevented it."

That last bit of admission knocked the winds right out of Anja's sails.

Rubbing the base of the neck, Vincent continued. "When I first left the well, I made a map."

"A map no one knows about," she volunteered.

"Actually," he corrected, "a map no one is supposed to know exists."

Anja thought about it for a second. "Why would you keep something like that a secret?"

"Just in case someone was desperate enough to want to go to the well." At that point, it was time for Vincent to start coming clean.

"Okay," he finally admitted. "I was looking for a buyer for the map. Someone who would pay a lot for the only copy."

Throwing her hands in the air, once again, "Same old Vincent. Of course, for the money," she exploded.

"Then why did you offer to help me. Are you getting something out of it?" Anja demanded, more furious at herself that she hoped things could be different.

"Not everyone was fortunate enough to have a caring family," looking at her. "Believe it or not, whether we're together or not, I think of Régine as family Always have."

That was true. Also, Vincent didn't ask for anything. He just wanted to help. There were many evenings Régine would ask Anja to call him, but she wouldn't. She couldn't.

"So we should be able to there and back pretty quick."

"What you don't seem to understand, I didn't memorize it," Vincent admitted. "Not really. I vaguely remember how to get there. The map was to give us a straight shot. Saving us time that we really could use."

"So what do we do now?" Anja asked him. "I'm not going to give up."

"We're not. I remember some of the routes," Vincent started, "not all of it. I can only hope that I can recognize the landmarks also. Right now, this is our best bet."

"I guess you're right," Anja nodded.

"Well, let's get going." Throwing the bundles on his shoulder, "I'll carry the bedrolls. You mind taking the food and water?"

Their trek started out from a parking field near the foot of the mountain. Looking up at the sky, Anja could see clouds rolling in .

"We may get a little wet," Anja said speaking to Vincent's back.

Taking notice, Vincent replied, "It looks like it's going to be a sun shower. It about to get very warm."

"This late in the year?" she asked.

"Yes. It's this area," Vincent started to explain. "The elemental witch and Well of Rites produce a mass amount of energy."

The hike continued for another three hours. It finished raining as they neared the last mountain. Even though Anja wanted to take a break, she kept quiet. Noticing her movements slowing down, Vincent made the call.

"Do you mind if we take a breather?" acting if he was exhausted. "Just ten minutes?"

Anja realized she worked up a deep drenching sweat. Silently, she was more than grateful to stop.

"I guess this is as good as a time to stop," she pointed out. Spotting a boulder to sit on, Anja removed her boots, massaging her feet and toes.

"I could help with that," Vincent offering his services.

"No, I'm good," she replied quickly.

Spying her putting her boots quickly back on, he instructed her to leave them off a little longer and flex. "We'll get moving in a bit," he informed her.

"We can go now," Anja stated.

"This is not your typical hike," Vincent explained. "We should be almost halfway now. We'll take another break once we get to the top."

Putting her on boots on, "the sooner we get there, the sooner we'll get that break."

Giving up, he helped her up, and they resumed their hike.

They stood in wonder as the high mountain towered before them. While the lower crossings were full of a rug of trees, green, red, orange and yellow, the summits were topped with ice. Without a word transpiring amid them, they knew it to be a sacred place.

"You feel it, don't you?" Vincent said to her.

The only life is a random bird, singing in a tree. Anja wants to pause to absorb in the noise. However, she has a very long hike in front of her.

"Yes," she barely whispered.

And so Anja and Vincent walked. Up the mountain, they went. Vincent walked like someone who'd been in some armed service; there was a marching quality to it. They walked those couple of hours not really talking. The lack of even small talk was bugging Anja, so she finally broke the silence.

"Just a thought," Anja wondered, "did you tell anyone where we were going or what are we doing?"

"It's ironic; I was pondering the same idea of you earlier."

"Someone probably put two and two together. Most people in town are aware of Régine's decline as well as my own. I don't think it would be a strong leap to come to a conclusion to where we would be going. Especially with our history."

"I had the very same thought. But no one and I mean no one," Vincent enunciated, "knew I had a map. I didn't have a need to sell it yet."

"I don't really believe in conscience," she pointed out. "If that's true, I think someone knew you had a map."

Despite the time of year, the morning was surprisingly warm, making the afternoon more so. Anja was ready to remove her jacket as they continued on.

"We need to proceed with caution, it's still a long way to get up there," Vincent said to her.

"Do you remember if this is the way?" Anja asked looking around the area.

Not wanting to worry her, he made minimal eye contact as he merely responded, "You know, this does look familiar."

Victor forgot Anja knew his facial tells. "You really don't seem sure."

"Five years have passed Anja," Vincent admitted nonchalantly. "Some things may have changed, some didn't."

Five years, Anja thought. That would have been about the time they stopped seeing each other.

"What happened that you would have had to make this journey, albeit dangerous?" Anja asked him as she touched her pendant.

Vincent once again changed the subject.

Rubbing the back of the neck, "Look, how about we get there first? Help you and your grandmother?"

Blinking, Anja quickly responded, "Is it that serious?"

With his lips pressed together, "It's just something I'd rather not talk about it."

"Okay," she muttered, backing off the subject.

Once again, they walked with simple small talk.

After continuing for another hour, Vincent decided to stop. Looking around, he could see things were not right.

"What's wrong?" asked Anja as she also took notice of the area.

"We've been traveling in the wrong direction," he admitted, not wanting to see the expression of disappointment in her eyes.

"Really?" Anja replied, "How long?"

"I don't know," staring at nothing. I believe there was a trio of trees we should have come to by now.

"A trio of trees?" she asked, looking at Vincent and the trees around them. "Three trees next to each other?"

"No," he quickly clarified. "I mean a tree with two trees growing from it. I remember thinking how cool it was."

"Okay," Anja sighed. "So there isn't a trio of trees. What does this mean?"

"Damn it!" Vincent swore as he surveyed the area once more.

"I'm sorry," he uttered. "It's not like I'm doing this on purpose. I haven't glanced at it since I first drew it. There never was a need to."

Setting her mouth set a hard line, "What can we do to try and find which way to go?"

"Look," Vincent began as he took a deep breath, "I'm quite sure we're close. I'm just not sure how far off we are."

"Hold on," Anja told him. Finding a spot to sit down, Anja pulled out her stones. "I'm going to try to cast a divination spell."

"Do you think something that simple will work?" Vincent asked her as he sat down beside her.

Touching her amulet, "It doesn't hurt to try."

In her dismay, as she sprinkled the powder, her magic fell flat. Anja's weakened state fizzled the spell once again. The desire to cry was overwhelming.

"What am I going to do?" she whispered.

"How about we try dowsing spell?" he tried to reassure Anja. "Maybe that will work."

"Maybe?" her lower lip trembled at the thought of having no powers.

"Don't give up Anja. It doesn't hurt to try," throwing her words back at her.

Anja gathered the necessary materials and began the spell. As a pendulum swings back and forth, it started to speed up and spin in a circle. The crystal finally shot off behind them.

"Of course," Vincent realized, "with this being a power spot, the Earth energies here is at its highest."

"There goes that idea!" Anja groaned to the fact they were lost.

Deciding to backtrack to where the trail broke off in three different directions they chose the path to the left. As they walked, Vincent realizes it was still the wrong way we have to go back.

"I'm sorry," he hesitated to tell Anja, "It must be the other trail. We, of course, pick the incorrect one."

"We're losing time. Vincent, we have got to get to the well."

"Please try and remember," Anja didn't want to sound frustrated, but she was. "Are you positive that is the direction to go?"

"It has to be" Vincent began. "It's the only way left." Pointing the way, he said, "let's go."

As they started on the trail, they saw another set of footprints. Vincent crouched down to get a better look at it. He could tell it was only a few hours old.

"Somebody's already been this way," Vincent said.

"I guess whoever took the map is going the right direction," Anja surmised.

"It's a good assumption." Vincent feeling had been correct. His concern now was just how dangerous was this person and how did they know he even had a map?

"So maybe we should follow their tracks," Anja suggested as she compared the size of the print with hers. "They should lead us straight to the well."

"If it was that easy," Vincent replied rubbing the back of his neck.

"It isn't?" Anja offered, wanting to get to the Well of Rites without any more delay.

"I don't know. Think about it," Vincent questioned. "How much of a lead did this mysterious person have on us?"

"If they left last night, they should be there," Anja spoke quietly.

"But," he quickly pointed out, "trying to make this hike is not only stupid, but it's also suicidal."

"So they left at first light with the map," Anja responded with a wrinkled brow. "Whoever it is, that person probably would be almost there."

"But this track is fairly recent," Vincent concluded. "They're ahead, but not as far ahead as they should be."

"So we should keep going?" she offered hopefully.

"For now, but we're going to have to stop soon," Vincent pointed out.

"Why?" Anja asked. "We should be on the correct path now."

"Yes we are," he stated. "However, we did lose time. It will be getting dark sooner than later and set up camp for the night will be more difficult."

"But what about Régine?" she maintained. "We're so close to finding it, Vincent."

"Not only is it unsafe, but we likewise can't take the chance of being turned around again during the dark." Vincent restated, "It would cost us even more time. We will get back to Régine before it's too late."

He could see she wasn't happy about it. Holding her shoulders, Vincent looked directly at her.

"We'll just set up camp have a good night's rest. I know your feet will be thankful for that. At first light, we will head out again. We will find the well, Anja. I promise."

"I'm going to hold you to it," Anja said somewhat doubtfully

"Of course, you will," he chuckled. His smile quickly faded as he began glancing about. "We're being followed."

Looking around, Anja saw nothing or no one. "Are you sure?"

"It's just a feeling I've been getting. Someone is out there. Not close though. It's as if whoever it is, knows to stay out of range."

Anja looked about, as she squinted. With her fading power, she couldn't sense anything or anyone.

"We're going to set up with our backs to this small shelter of woods. This way we are not entirely exposed." As an afterthought, Vincent said, "Also, no fire. We don't want to signal anyone."

"So we're not having a hot meal?" she mumbled.

"Not tonight," Vincent sympathized with her. "Sorry."

Anja unpacked her bedroll and placed it under the makeshift tent Vincent created. She was beginning to feel the wear on her back.

"No time to complain," she thought. "Régine needs me to succeed."

It was at that moment she began to feel a bit light headed. Vincent quickly caught her.

"Are you okay?" Vincent asked before she collapsed.

"Yes," Anja stammered "Fine. Just a little dizzy. I might be a little dehydrated."

Vincent sat her pack on the ground. "Sit. Drink some water and eat something. I have some dried meat here. Don't fight; just let me take care of you."

"Okay." Anja conceded as she took a long drink of water. Anja didn't realize precisely how dry her throat was.

Vincent was surprised Anja gave in without a fight. Things were looking better.

"I'm really not one to eat this." she began holding the dried meat in her hand. After taking a bite, "it's really not as bad as I thought."

Shrugging his shoulders, "You never know unless you give things a chance."

"Régine always said that," Anja whispered. Tears started to well in her eyes as she sniffed.

"I'm sorry," was all he could think to say to her.

"Vincent," she began with a trembling chin "what if we don't get to the well in time? What am I going to do? I can't live without Régine."

The emotions finally broke through. Quickly turning her head, Anja didn't want Vincent to see her weak as she quietly sobbed. The movement of her shoulders gave it away.

Vincent pulled her into his arms to comfort her. It felt right to have her there. He had to warn himself not to take advantage of the situation.

"I know you will get through this," stroking her hair as he attempted to reassure her. "I know it as a fact. We will not go back without being able to restore Régine."

"You actually believe that?" Anja questioned, wiping her nose with a tissue.

"There is one fact I know about you, Anja Shields. You are a stubborn woman. Whatever demands to be done, you do it. I guess it attracted me to you long ago."

Realizing she was still in his arms, Anja quickly rose as she touched her amulet, "I am all Régine has so of course, I will do anything to save her."

"I know." Realizing the moment was over, Vincent changed the subject. "Want some more dried meat?"

Not wanting to tell him she found the dried meat disgusting, "I wouldn't mind some of the bread if we have any left."

"There's plenty. And make sure you have enough to drink," Vincent reminded her as he gave Anja a bottle.

Stretching out her legs, Anja took a deep breath before biting into the hunk of bread. With her mouth full, she asked, "When we get to the Well of Rites, just what should I expect?"

"The elemental witch will first have to deem you worthy of the sacred water," Vincent said as he stroked his jaw.

"You were actually deemed worthy?" she asked perplexed.

A pronounced sigh passed his lips. "This is not about me. We're talking about what you will go through."

As Anja touched her amulet, she asked him, "What if I'm not deemed worthy?"

"First, don't think like that. You are one of the truest people I've ever met. Male or female. You will not have a problem." Stretching, he knew it was time to turn in. "Let's get some sleep. Tomorrow will be a big day."

"Good night, Vincent," she yawned and went to sleep as she questioned whether he was right.

* * *

The stranger remained hidden just outside of Vincent's magic barrier. It was no surprise that Vincent would try to strengthen his barrier, it but it wasn't going to help. Pulling out several herbs, incense and a string of black Amethyst, the stranger began a chant. As the smoke rose, the stones became a snake and began to burrow under the ground slowly. Reaching its destination inside the shield, it waited.

The stranger blew smoke into the small burrow, directing it towards Anja. Once it was evident, she took in a deep breath, inhaling it all, the stranger smiled.

"You will sleep like a stone, Anja," the stranger whispered.

Slithering towards Anja, the stones slowly wrap its tail around the amulet, pulling it over her head. With the amulet now in its possession, the stone snake returned to its master.

"Now I'm ready," the stranger smiled while placing the amulet in the satchel with the map.

Chapter Seven

Vincent's body was sore when he woke. He tried to recall what was on the map. He never expected to have a need to come back. Now, in hindsight, he wished he looked at it more.

Still lying on his back, he called her in a hushed tone. "Anja. Anja, wake up. We need to get moving."

Vincent rose from the ground. Looking towards the small tent, he saw how peaceful Anja looked sleeping. He actually didn't want to rouse her, but he knew he had to.

"Anja. Come on now." Stepping into his boots, he glanced back, noticing how still she was.

Reaching inside, he touched her cheek. Vincent could feel how cold her skin was.

"Anja!" he almost shouted. Shaking her, she finally woke up.

"What?" she began, feeling grumpy. Opening her eyes, Anja saw Vincent hovering over her. "I'm up. I'm up."

"How do you feel?" he asked.

"Tired," she confessed. "Feels like I just fell asleep."

"Anja, you've slept almost ten hours." Taking a closer look are her, "Your powers seem to be waning even faster."

Anja groaned as she turned. "I'm just so tired, Vincent." She merely wanted to go back to sleep.

"I know," Vincent began as he handed her a bottle. "Anja, here's some water. We need to get moving, but..."

"No," she murmured, as she sat up, pulling the blanket with her. "I am not going to slow us down. We need to hurry."

Looking at her state of undress, Vincent stammered, suddenly feeling a bit warm. "You need to get ready. I'll wait outside for you."

"Okay," Anja replied, not wanting to look at him. "I'll be as quick as I can."

Clearing his throat, "I'll figure out how long it should take for us to get to the Well of Rites."

Anja watched Vincent walk away. Taking a deep breath, Anja knew there was no way to deny it. She was getting weaker. Somehow, she will find the strength to keep going. Anja took a few moments before exiting. Looking around, Vincent was nowhere to be seen.

"Vincent?" she called out, gathering up the supplies. Anja wanted to be ready to go as soon as he returned. It didn't take long to get all the gear was ready to go, but Vincent still wasn't in sight.

"Vincent!" Anja still heard nothing.

Scanning across the area, she saw what looked to be his cap. Walking towards it, Anja barely heard the call of her name. It was from Vincent. Straining to listen, she heard him again.

Looking over the edge, Anja could see him lying on the ground twenty feet down. Slowly, she made her way down the overhang to him. The terrain going down was littered with large stones. Anja was doing her best not to twist an ankle.

"Oh, my goddess. Vincent," she cried finally reaching him. "What happened?"

"What happened is," cursing at himself, "I was trying to figure out which direction we should go. I think I lost my footing and fell down this embankment."

Sitting up, Vincent winced it pain. His face seemed to lose color.

"You're seriously hurt!" she exclaimed.

"I know. Anja, I'm sorry." Vincent began to cough. "I think I make have broken a rib or two."

With wide eyes, Anja saw the blood being spit up. It was then she knew and whispered, "This is bad, Vincent."

Vincent saw the fear in her eyes. "I know, and I'm sorry Anja. I don't think I'm going to make it any further. Not right now."

Time was something they didn't have in abundance. Neither did Régine. Anja knew what she had to do. Something she didn't want to do with anyone. However with the situation at hand, not doing it was not an option. Without Vincent, there would be no way she could get to the Well of Rites. Ignoring her heart, she told herself he was the only one who could help her save Régine.

"Listen, Anja began, pulling an embellished vial with an S stamped on it, from her pocket, "Régine gave this to me long ago."

Squinting his eyes, Vincent looked at the vial she held. "What is that?"

"It's my first tears," Anja explained to him. "It is combined with tears of my mother and Régine. Their tears of joy at my birth."

"I've heard of these vials," he said. "The tears of a water witch are said to be quite powerful."

"Yes, especially the first tears, combined with those of my family's love. It's only to be used in the direst time magic was needed." Anja whispered, "If only they were powerful enough to revive Régine."

"It would have been a temporary fix, Vincent noted, remembering what he read about this type of magic.

"Primarily it's the last resort to be taken." Anja shook her head, "I believe that's where we're at."

"It's very potent, Anja," Vincent reminded her. "It's also binding."

Anja looked at Vincent. She could sense the pain radiating from him in waves.

"I'm going to use my family's magic you to save you," Anja made up her mind. "Without you, this journey ends. Régine will die, and I will follow."

"Do you understand what will happen if you use this on me?" Placing his hand in Anja's lap, "It will bind you to me. Me to you," stressing on the last point, "for life. I don't think that is something you really want to do, not with you mistrusting me."

"Vincent, I am the reason you are here now. Why you are hurt. Even with our past, you are willing to help me. I can't take the chance you may die because of it." Tears shimmered in Anja's eyes, "It's too much."

Vincent began wincing in pain as he attempted to grab the vial, "I can't let you do this."

Anja opened the vial quickly before he could stop her or she'd change her mind. She applied the tears to his wounds for the quickest absorption. "Too late, Vincent. It's already done."

"Damn it, Anja," Vincent swore. "It's not what you want!"

"You are my only chance to get to the well, and save Régine," she told Vincent. "I will do whatever it takes."

Vincent could feel his powers boosting the tears' powers even more. With the use of the tears, his wounds were completely healed. His ribs quickly moved back in place. As he lay there, Vincent could see flashes of Anja's life. The lonely girl she once was. The bond she has with Régine. The emotions Anja felt, he felt.

When the first surge of power went through him, Vincent had to catch his breath to sit up. Staring at Anja, he fully understood what she did, and why. Bound or not, once their journey was completed, he was going to win her back.

"Thank you," he whispered to her. "I know the cost to you is tremendous."

He kissed her, and the world slipped away, forgetting all of their problems. It was slow and delicate, exhilarating in ways that words would never be. His hand paused below her ear, his thumb stroking her cheek as their gasps merged. She spread her fingers down his spine, drawing him closer till she could feel the beating of his heart next to her breast.

It became apparent that their love was still there, It sat there, just beneath the surface. Waiting to bloom once again Vincent was bound to her in the flesh and Spirit. Thoughts of being with Anja possessed his mind.

"Why are you staring?" Vincent asked.

A sad smile played on her lips. Anja didn't want to admit she missed him. To do so may open her up to being burned again. It took her years to lessen the pain of her walking away.

Vincent pulled her down to him under the tree. He had missed her too.

"Believe me; it wasn't easy staying far from you. But I have it deep inside of my soul that we are bound for eternity." Indicating his heart, "you are always here for me. I love you." He moved closer to her.

Anja knew she wouldn't have control over her emotions in a short while. Her heart raced as he leaned on her back. His voice was broken and husky. She could feel his soul in them. He loved her.

He said nothing. He just stared into Anja's fiery eyes. Her brown-mahogany eyes glittered with a naughty glimmer. They glow with humor and playfulness that never seem to escape her eyes.

With his palms, Vincent cupped her face and moved closer, "you saved my life. I owe you everything."

She licked her lips fortifying herself in response, but she hadn't been fast enough.

The moment she was about to speak, he closed in with his mouth. At once, Vincent's hard and wet mouth crashed upon hers. She melted like butter upon the flame. Anya knew this is what she's been missing. This is what she gave up.

Anja quickly removed her clothes. At that moment, Vincent was all she could see.

His eyes flamed with desire as he stared at her nakedness.

"You are so beautiful," he flicked his tongue against her delicate ears.

Anja blushed as her eyes traveled to the bulge in his trousers. Without warning, he swept her into his arms and carried her to a small copse of trees.

She closed her eyes and awaited his touch, with her body, throbbing in all the right places.

He glanced at her attractive body one last time, and whispered, "You're mine forever."

Vincent lowered his lips to the caramel mounds on her chest. He swallowed a diamond-hard nipple easily and fed upon it. The sensation from his lips started an inferno that couldn't be extinguished until her desires were fed.

A moan escaped her lips as Vincent's other hand started a journey from the swell of her breasts to the valley of her belly. She knew where his hands were going, and she yearned for them to meet that hidden grove between her legs. She felt her juices spill against her laps.

Vincent had been the one man who could make her body reacts this way. He knew the right places to touch. Vincent is the only man who ever understood her completely.

"Ahh..." Anja moaned and arched her hips upwards as his hands brushed the curly hair on her Venus mound.

It wasn't long before he slipped a finger into her wetness. Slowly, he found the tight pleasure bud between the walls of her womanhood. He pressed a finger against it and began to rub gently.

"Vincent..." Anja moaned as his fingers danced inside of her, while his wet mouth sucked her nipples. She was drowning in a sea of desire. She was going mad from too much pleasure.

Vincent ignored her cries, knowing she would find release soon enough. He loved the way she responded to his touches. Vincent slipped a finger between her slippery folds.

It didn't take long before he pulled his jeans off and set his huge cock free.

Anja's heart began a wild race as she stared at his pleasure rod.

"I love you, Anja."

"I love you, Vincent," she whispered in a weak voice. "I never stopped."

Vincent's cock was so much longer and more substantial than his fingers, but the tight fit only forced her to moan more. Wiggling her hips, Anja wanted to accept all of him at once. He drove deep inside of her filling her completely.

"I want to be the only man to make you scream," Vincent whispered to her.

Anja let out a cry at the feeling of her body stretching to accommodate his girth and deep penetration.

"You have succeeded," she countered attempting not to giggle.

Anja buried her nose against his throat as Vincent thrust hard slamming her against the door repeatedly.

Extreme pleasure swept through Anja, making her even wetter. She shuddered to feel her climax approaching with each of his driving thrusts.

Anja shoved her fingers in his hair and used her hold to force his mouth to her breast. His tongue brushed Anja's tender swollen nipple.

Vincent slowed his hard thrusts to one last deep penetration until he remained buried entirely. Anja's body was rippling in desire. Shaking for release as Vincent was rock hard inside her.

Anja gasped, clutching her legs even tighter around his waist. She gripped his hair tighter and demanded even more.

Vincent's reply was a low noise in his throat. He pressed his body fully against her applying pressure to Anja sensitive nub.

Anja's breathing turned eager, and her body shook. Her heart softened when she noticed Vincent was holding back for her. Giving Anja precisely what she asked for. More. Vincent rolled his hips against her body.

Anja's vision blurred at the sheer combination of pleasure and ecstasy he created. She gripped him close, whimpering in pleasure as wave after wave of sexual tremors broke through her core, shattering her body in a tide of unimaginable happiness. Anja clenched her body tight, moving with him to take in every single thrust of his aggressive possession. When Vincent groaned against her neck and continued pushing, she almost fell apart. Anja rode the feeling as long and as hard as she could until her body quit moving out of complete exhaustion.

Chapter Eight

Vincent stared into the sky, his arms wrapped about Anja as she rested. Lying here like this, she appeared so exposed. She was light and delicate. He was so bewitched by her.

"Anja?"

"Yes," she murmured.

He knew she could be strong if she had to be. He'd observe her resolve more than once. Still, would it be enough to sustain her if she discovered the truth about him, about everything?

"Do you know what it was I wanted when I came to the well?" he asked turning towards her.

"You said it was power," Anja responded.

"Yes, it's true. I wanted power." Vincent folded his arms behind his head. "It wasn't exactly what I bargained for."

"There was more?" she asked.

"I wanted power, but it was power not to feel pain."

"I don't understand."

"When you left it created a deep hole inside of me. It was like a never-ending dark void that consumed everything. I felt nothing. Empty. I could never understand why you felt we were wrong," Vincent's mouth set in a hard line. "I never wanted to feel that again."

"I knew you were hiding something and it made trusting you difficult."

"I know that now," a muscle in his jaw twitched. "But back then I didn't understand. I didn't want to. I do now."

"You do?"

"Yes. This is the story of Vincent Salazar."

Anja turned onto her side to face him. Her face shone in the filtered sunlight. "Tell me," she whispered.

"Growing up I lived in a group home. There were seven of us all in one bedroom. Our foster mother, Kris, didn't care about us. All she wanted was the money she was given. Whether we were fed, whether we had clothes or was sick, she didn't care. The older kids, which I was one, resorted to the old five finger discount. Usually, it was just bread and peanut butter, but it was enough to get the younger ones by."

"That's horrible." sadness clouded her features.

"One day, Darrin, who was like a little brother to me, got sick. Really sick, it was pneumonia ... and died."

"Where was your foster mother, uh Kris?"

Shrugging his shoulders. "Probably with her new boyfriend. Protecting herself, she told the authorities we had been covering for each other and never realized that Darrin was sick. She was scared to lose her paycheck. We were put back in the system until we aged out."

Anja's eyes glimmered with watery tears. She felt her heart breaking for the youth that was stolen from him. Placing her hand to his chest, Anja could feel his heart beating quicker.

"When you left me, it felt the same. Once more, I was alone. I didn't want to feel that way ever again. The feeling of powerless against anything or anyone."

"But you're not powerless."

"The thing that I gave the witch was your picture. The only picture I had of you that I held onto."

"So you came to the well because of me? Because I hurt you?"

"Turns out, you didn't hurt me. I just didn't understand. I was afraid to tell you the truth of where I came from."

"It was the only thing then made me walk away."

"I know, but I want you back. I've always wanted you back."

"I don't know Vincent. Right now it's more about Régine. I can't think about myself, as much as I want to. Even more so now that we are bound."

"You can do both." Vincent pointed out to her. "We can do both."

"I believe we can."

"I'll hold you to that."

"I know you will. And Vincent?"

"Yeah?"

"Thank you. Thank you for telling me. Vincent, I never wanted to hurt you."

"I know. It was just my defense mechanism. I didn't know if I could trust you. The same way you didn't know if you could believe or trust me."

Vincent drew her against his chest. As his nose nuzzled her ear, Anja made a tiny gasp. She felt his lips softly brush her slim neck. Her face burned.

Vincent helped her up. Seeing that Anja was feeling uncomfortable, he turned his back to her giving her some sense of privacy as they both dressed.

Anja picked up the vial to place in her bag. While she was replacing the stopper, one lone drop fell on her hand. As it was quickly absorbed, a boost of strength and energy ran through her body.

As they headed back to their site, even Vincent noticed how much more energetic her pace was.

"Are you feeling okay?"

"I feel stronger if that is what you're asking."

"What happened?"

"A single drop was absorbed into my skin."

"Do you mind if I check you real quick?"

"If you feel it is necessary, go ahead."

"Well, you do seem a bit stronger."

"I know. Maybe all I needed was the tears to give me back my powers."

"It is a temporary fix, Anja. You're stronger, but I can feel it rising and dipping. If anything, that single tear gave you more time. We will still have to get to the Well of Rites."

"Okay, let's get our gear together and get moving. We need to hurry for Régine's sake."

Walking back she asked, "Do you know which way we need to go?"

"Yes, if I remember correctly, this way towards the west. There should be a small lake. We'll be very close."

"Thank the Goddess," Anja murmured as she began to touch her amulet. Feeling across her chest, Anja no longer felt it.

"Vincent. My amulet is missing."

Looking around where they just laid, on her hands and knees, Anja searched the ground.

"No, no, no," she cried

"Anja, you said you don't take it off," Vincent responded.

"I don't," Anja stressed. "How could this have happened? It's been around my neck since we left."

"Did it have a loose clasp on it? It could have fallen off during the night or after we…"

Trying not to let her voice shrill, Anja calmly spoke, "There is no clasp. I was wearing it last night. It was around my neck, and now it's gone."

"Did you notice it missing this morning?"

"No, Anja admitted. I was concerned with you. I actually didn't think of it."

Walking further out from their small camp, to the tall grass, Vincent could see a trail. No bigger than a foot wide, the flattened was made by someone or something. From there, he spotted a hole. Could have been made by an animal, but since it also led straight to where Anja slept, Vincent doubted it.

"Damn it!" Vincent swore.

"What do you see?" Anja asked as he walked back.

Blowing out a breath, "Someone was here."

"How?" Anja questioned, looking at Vincent. "I'm a pretty light sleeper."

"Yes, but" he quickly pointed out, "it was tough to wake you this morning."

Realization hit her. "That's how it was taken. Do you think someone could have used a spell?"

"I'm almost positive that they did," agreeing with her as he ran his hands down his face. "I know one thing for sure."

"What's that?" she asked, wondering if things were as bad as they seemed.

"We need to get to the Well of Rites, now."

"Because they are on their way there now," Anja realized.

"Yes. If we're lucky, we'll catch up to the thief."

"Right now, we need another plan in case we don't. Without the amulet," Vincent explained, "you have nothing to pay the witch."

"So what do you suggest we do?" Anja began. "I have nothing left."

"I think we should combine our powers," answered Vincent.

"Combine our powers?" Anja repeated. "Do you know what that would mean? What it would mean to me?"

"Yes," Vincent looked at her. "I do know."

"Combining powers is one thing, but you add in the vial of tears…"

"It would give me power over you. I know" Vincent looked at her, "But once you drink the water, it will dissipate."

Anja thought. Once again, she knew that she would do anything for her Régine.

"Okay, let's do it if we have to, she said to him. We may not have any other choice."

The mountain trail was merely the least challenging climb over the rocky boulders. Several of the rocks stood so high before them, they forced Anja and Vincent to climb up on all fours. They lost momentum each time their knapsacks would shift, almost pulling them back down. After approximately an hour, they were almost to the end of their destination.

The outside of the cavern is majestic. Steep inclines of up to 200 feet tall, rise like a natural wall. The massive stones, with marbling of white veins through its dark color, dominate the area. Even though the temperature was dropping, Anja was in awe of the sight.

The cavern did nothing but channel the cold air. So much so, the chill wind tugged at Vincent and Anja's clothing and whipped the loose hair about their faces. It surprised Anja at the sudden drop of temperature. She wrapped her arms tighter around herself, pulling her jacket secured and tucking her chin down into her sweater.

It was a cave entrance of eternal blackness, as they stepped in, their shadows dissolved into the neighboring dark. It was humid. The only noise was trickling water.

"We have to move slowly," Vincent began, "keeping our backs to the wall. Any misstep could plunge us into the deep chasm of the cavern."

"I'll be careful," Anja whispered

Moving around by following the clammy wall of the cave with their hands, suddenly, bright flaming torches came to life, illuminating the shaft before them and covering the entire cavern in a flickering bright glow.

"We found it," Vincent said.

"Thank the Goddess," Anja replied. "Let's go in."

"Wait not yet."

Standing at the mouth of a hidden cave, they finalized their plan. Moving slowly, Anja and Vincent made their way to the well keeping their backs to the wall. Any misstep could plunge them into the deep chasm of the cavern.

Finally, when they reach the center, everything seemed to go quiet. The Well of Rites stood before them.

A deep feeling of serenity overcame her as she gazed in ecstasy at the expanse of color that fell before her. Anja was the first to see the Well of Rites. An octagonal platform covered its actual display. It was golden, and there were magical inscriptions written all over.

"It's beautiful," Anja exclaim barely above a whisper.

"That it is," Vincent agreed, "But something is not right. The water isn't flowing, and the witch is always by the well."

"Do you think we should combine our magic now?" Anja asked as she moved towards the well.

"I think we should," he said. "I'm getting an uneasy feeling."

Taking her hand into his, "This is your last chance, Anja. Are you sure about this?"

"The only thing I'm sure of is saving Régine." she whispered.

They took each other hands. Concentrating, Vincent builds his power to overtake Anja's. The energy that begins to build in her was more than Vincent expected, but at this point, they needed all the power.

Once their magic was combined, they readied themselves to access the Well of Rites. At that moment, they both were knocked on their asses.

The witch rose from the well. Her movements seemed to mirror the rhythm of the water.

This fair skinned creature seems to have a cold-hearted feel about her. As cold as the water she sprang from. Her lips curled in a mocking smile. With knee length white hair, her vivid pink eyes didn't give Vincent a second look. Her demeanor changed when it came to Anja. The witch stared intensely at Anja.

"I am Xalena. The keeper of the sacred water. Why have you come to the Well of Rites?"

"You're on," Vincent whispered as he stepped back into the shadows.

Doing her best to steady her shaky voice, "I am Anja Shields,"

"Please step forward Anja Shields."

"I have come for the healing water for my grandmother Régine. She's dying, and her magic is fading."

Xalena dissolved into a golden mist. Seconds later, reappearing directly in front of Anja. She was looking for any sign of deception.

"I see you are also fading with your magic. Why would you save her and not yourself?"

"Régine is my heart. There is nothing I wouldn't do for her. She is the only mother I have ever known."

"I can see your words are true."

"They are."

"I will give you the water to heal your grandmother."

Anja's eyes opened wide, "Thank you very much."

"Your request is selfless," Xalena began, "I will also give you the water to heal yourself."

"Thank you," Anja cried. Thank you.

"What do you bring a sacrifice?"

Blowing out a breath, and then looking at Vincent, Anja spoke clearly.

"I had in my possession an aquamarine amulet which belonged to my mother who died when I was a baby. It was stolen, and now I have nothing."

"Then nothing is what you will with."

Tears streamed down Anja's face. "Please. We have gone through so much to get here."

"The journey is meant to be difficult. It shows the determination of the seeker."

"I can't leave without the water." Anja finally breaks down and cry. "I can't leave empty handed."

"You should have brought an offering," Xalena

"She said it was stolen," Vincent said stepping forward.

"That is not my concern," Xalena stated, now standing in front of Vincent.

"What are we going to do Vincent? We need the water. I can't let Régine die. I just can't."

Vincent looked into her eyes. He knew Anja was more concerned for Régine than her own self. This is the woman he wants in his life. Vincent knew right at that moment, what they were going to do.

"We do it the hard way, Anja. We take it!"

Chapter Nine

"You annoy me. Get away from the well before it is too late." Xalena's features became stern.

Without wasting time, he closed the distance between where they stood and the witch. It was a dangerous move, as he could drop into the chasm, but he dared. Anja stopped right in front of the witch.

"We're not leaving without the water."

Before the witch could say a word, Anja released her fist and punched her in the face. Blood trickled down from the witch's nostrils. Now that her blood has been spilled, Xalena could no longer teleport. She grabbed Anja's neck tightly and raised her into the air.

"You are not even a challenge!" She smiled.

"Let's see how you'll stop us both?" Vincent taunted.

Vincent harnessed his powers and also jumped to the other side.

"Vincent!" Anja called out. Get the water!

A glint of light caught Anja's eye. She failed to notice the dagger the witch had taken out of her garment.

The witch's dark nails clawed tightly to the knife. Without warning, she fired Anja a punch in the abdomen and sliced through the muscle of her arm.

"Ahh!" Anja cried the pain made her stumble, and she fell hard.

Vincent stilled as he realized what had happened.

"Anja! Get away from her!" He yelled and launched a kick at her, but the witch was faster. She could see his plan, so she was careful to avoid it.

Angrily, she harnessed the power of the wind. The debris that lay on the floor was lifted and began to spin like a dust storm. Anja wards herself from as many as she could.

"I warned you boy..." with a finger pointed at him, she raised him and moved him towards the direction of the chasm.

"No!" Anja cried.

A power erupted from within Anja. Vincent fell to the ground two feet before falling to his death. Xalena was thrown from the well and down the chasm. Without the power of Xalena, the Well of Rites shut itself down.

"We need to get out of here." Vincent urged. "The witch will be back."

"But we're so close," Anja looked at the Well.

"Without the witch, there is no magic water. Come on, you're hurt badly."

Totally frustrated, she gave in, "Damn it!"

"Let me help you up."

Anja chastised herself. It was easier than breaking down and crying because she was the cause of Régine not getting the water .

"I've failed," Anja had no choice but to face the facts. Régine was going to die as well as herself.

"How's your arm?" Vincent asked as he attempted to get a good look at it.

"It's healing. Not as fast as I would like it to."

As Vincent gazed at Anja, it drove every ounce of air from her lungs. Bending his head down towards her, the fall of stones got their attention.

"Did you hear that? Someone's coming," she whispered.

"Shh." Vincent pulled her back into the shadows, holding her.

The steps came closer to them. They could see it was a young woman. This young woman was holding the map.

"Stop!" Vincent said coming from the darkness. "You stole that from me."

"I don't know what you're talking about," she claimed. She quickly darted by trying to escape, "Now if you excuse me."

"Vincent," Anja pointed out, "if she has the map, she may also have the amulet."

"That exactly what I was thinking," Vincent replied taking a better look at the young woman ran.

The young woman quickly made her way into the cavern. They immediately ran after her.

"You have my amulet. I know you do."

"Still, don't know what you're talking about, she replied not looking back."

"Anja, doesn't she look familiar to you?"

The tan-skinned young woman, standing 5' 7" tall, has a resolute sense about her. Her face is lean including a cleft chin, a well-formed nose, and angled lips. Her brown eyes are deep set, and she has smooth eyebrows. Her long and wavy, coffee-colored locs were pulled up.

"I can't say for certainty, but I am confident that I saw you when we arrived at the motel."

"Really?" she asked arching an eyebrow, looking for a means to escape. "I'm sure I don't know what you are talking about."

"Yes, smart mouth. If you want to tail someone, try a hairstyle that doesn't stand out." It was then Anja saw the stone twinkling and knew for sure.

Throwing her fire magic at them, the girl gets turned around and runs further into the cave.

"We can't let her get away," Anja spoke. "I have to get my amulet back."

The girl runs as quickly as she can, making another wrong turn. The wrong turn ends up having her face to face with a wall. At this point, she's desperate, like a caged animal. She poses herself ready for a fight.

"Nowhere to go," Vincent said with Anja close behind him.

"Look, I've come too far to be stopped now. I'm sorry I took this from you. Truly I am."

As she threw her fire magic directly at Vincent, Anja quickly threw her hands up casting a protection spell to help Vincent. It absorbed some of its energy.

"I will not let you get away with the map or my mother's amulet. You will die before I allow it."

Anja knew her magic would last for long, but once Vincent added his own, she threw everything they had into it. Slowly, the girl was forced back.

"Stop!" she screamed. "Please stop!"

They halted their assault, leaving Anja breathing hard. But she refuses to show any weakness.

"I'm sorry," the young woman began, "but I need these items. It's the only way I can save my mother."

"Why should I care about your mother?" Anja looked at her in disbelief. "I am trying to save my grandmother. A woman who raised me."

"Because my mother," the young woman explained, "is also your mother."

"That's impossible," Anja emphasized. "My mother is dead."

"No," she assured Anja. "Our mother is very much alive. I am your sister."

"You lie!" Anja exploded. "You want me to think that my mother would have me believe she was dead all this time? She would not be that cruel."

"Believe me or don't believe me, but it's true. Here is the vial of tears our mother gave me. To use as a last resort."

Anja looked at the vial. It was identical to the one she possesses. Right down to the "S" symbol.

"I don't believe it," Anja muttered.

"You can believe it. Our mother is alive."

Looking at Vincent, "Could this be true?"

Vincent looked closely at both women. Yes, there was a similarity, but he knew there was one way to be sure. Pulling his stones from his pouch, he examined the young woman. She stood there keeping a watchful eye on Anja.

"Well?" Anja asked anxiously.

"It's true, Anja," finishing his scan. "This young woman is your sister. Your energy is nearly the same."

Anja was floored. How could this happen? Her life has just been turned upside down in just minutes.

"Look, my name is Katie Ellison. I'm a fire elemental."

"Fire? So we do not have the same father?"

"No. Our mother married my father years later. It only since the attack that she was finally willing to tell me about you. Everything."

"Which is?"

"Our mother has been in hiding since you were born. She's been trying to escape a villainous thief who is draining, no stealing witches' powers. Mother was scared for her life, for your life. It was my father who also helped her."

"How are you not affected?"

"When my father learned I was on the way, he made this journey. He knew one day he would not be here for me. It was his way of keeping me safe."

"Who was she hiding from?"

"I'm sorry to tell you Anja, but it's your father."

"My father? First, you tell me that my mother is alive! That I have a sister! Now you tell me that person who is draining the powers from witches and even killing them is my father? What am I supposed to think?"

"I know it's something mother regrets every day. Letting you believe she was dead. Your father would kill you if he even knew of your existence."

"But why?" Anja emphasizing it was a lot to take in.

"Until Mother saw the man, he really was thought she was in love. She refused to be bound to him. A child between them would be powerful. A child more powerful than both of them."

"This is a fantastic story. I've never been powerful," Anja insisted. "Never."

"Yes, I know," Katie was hoping Anja would believe her. "Everything I've said is true."

"Did Régine know?" Anja asked.

"Anja," Katie started, "what is important is..."

"Damn it!" she snapped. With her eyes ablaze, Anja asked once more. "Did Régine know that my mother is alive?"

Katie whispered, "Yes."

"Did she know about you?" Anja asked even though in her heart, she knew the answer.

"Yes, but we've never met. Mother knew it would be too dangerous."

Anja walked away. She really didn't want to hear any more.

"Katie," Vincent interjected. "Give her a few minutes. Please finish."

"Our mother had placed a strong protection over Anja and grandmother, but with her powers waning, the protections failed. Because of this, she became susceptible to an attack."

"So, if Azeal had never started attacking the witches, he would have never known about Anja."

"What is it that he wants?"

"Power plain and simple. That's all he ever wanted. He knew how powerful our mother is and he knew a child with her with be even more powerful. He didn't want to take the chance a child they produce to be swayed by our mother's influence. That child would have the power to destroy him."

Vincent put his arm around her shoulder, "I think Régine was trying to protect. To keep you happy and safe. Especially with not have either of your parents in your life."

"What else Katie?"

"Mom had you in secret. This was after she learned exactly who and what your father is. She has to hide you as a baby and flee." Sitting down, Katie continued.

"So not only is my mother alive, but the person who is attacking the witches is my father. To make things worse, he wants me dead."

"Again," Katie whispered, "I am sorry."

"If you really came here to help our mother and you've already been here. Why are you still here?"

"Because I was not worth the deemed worthy to receive it."

"Because you stole the items that you now possess."

"Yes that's true I thought maybe you would find a way to get the water and then I would just simply take it from you."

"That wouldn't have happened. We're here to save Régine."

"But what about our mother?"

"You know if you would have just asked we would have helped you," Vincent said. "Instead of you stealing from us."

"I didn't know whether or not I could trust you to help me. My mother is all that I have in this world."

"I know exactly how you feel," said Anja. "I would do anything for Régine even give up a mother's amulet. But if I knew I had a sister and that sister thought the mother she cried for at night was actually alive, raising another child. I would have said something. I would have asked for help."

"Anja," Vincent said. "It's done. We can't change the past. All we can do is move on. You've helped me see that."

Not wanting to upset Anja more, Katie asked, "So what do we do now?"

Taking a deep breath, Anja announced, "We go back and confront the elemental witch maybe the three of us she will give us the water."

"We can help not only Régine but our mother also," Katie added.

The three of them walk back into the cavern the witch was waiting for them.

Chapter Ten

Xalena exclaimed, "You again? Why would you return? I have denied the three of you already; you will not change my mind."

"Yes but I now have the amulet I am willing to give you to save my mother's life to save Régine's life."

"Yes but you are here with a thief who already shows no honor that makes you just as bad as she is."

"Please we've come so far we cannot leave empty-handed."

"I'll say this one last time. Leave now! Go before I have to kill you all." Xalena's voiced boomed.

"Like she said," Vincent began, "we've come a long way. You have to know what's going on with the witches losing their powers."

"I am well aware, and that is not my concern besides he doesn't want you to gain your powers."

"He? He who?" Anja questioned.

"Why, your father of course. Once he found out that you actually existed, he knew you'd come here. It was he who gave your sister the information that a map existed."

"I knew you were too good to be true!" Anja accused Katie. "More lies!"

"No, it was a spell I cast to find a way to get here." Looking at Anja, "I swear! I didn't know."

"Of course she didn't know. That was the plan. Azrail doesn't want you to regain your powers. You, your mother and grandmother will all die for the deception."

"My own father wants me dead?"

"Of course. You were never to be born. Now that you are you are more of a threat to Azrail than ever, you can't be allowed to live."

"It can't be."

"What you don't seem to understand is that your father, Azrail, is the most powerful warlock of all time. The vision that he saw. The way things can be for witches. You should be happy that you have such a father."

"I'm really not."

"I know to find out that your father actually prefers you didn't exist has to be a blow to you. In the end, it will be what's best for us all." Xalena stood behind her, whispering, "He will change everything. What are a few dead witches to achieve such a vision?"

"You sound like you're in love with him."

"Maybe I am, or maybe I know it's better to be with him than against him. He's already made the sacrifice needed for my loyalty."

"You know I'm not going to let that happen. I will stop Azrail."

"You don't even have the power to help yourself. How are you going to fight him?"

Katie stood shoulder to shoulder with Anja.

"Because now she has a sister. She's not in this alone."

"She also has me," Vincent said. "Remember, I've already been here. My powers will not diminish."

"That is true." Xalena moved in circles around the well. "That power is the only reason why you're still alive."

Moving directly in front of him, Xalena looked Vincent in the eyes.

"I had someone go out to make sure that you never made it here. The fools failed. You were fortunate. Very lucky indeed."

Xalena moved back to the well, staring at the three of them.

Anja understood, "so you're the reason he fell down that embankment. It wasn't a simple accident."

"Yes. I did not have the foresight to know that you would sacrifice your tears for this man."

"So you were never going to give me the water?"

"No, I wasn't." Taking a deep breath, Xalena's smile grew. "Sorry. You were to die. Just like your mother, grandmother. Dead. If you somehow made it here, I was to send you on your way, empty-handed. Then you would die."

"Anja, we're not going to get anywhere with her."

"You're right, Vincent. We're just going to have to take the water."

The cavern trembled as Xalena laughed. "I've already knocked you down once. Do you really want to tempt fate? I can guarantee you will not make it out of here. None of you. You will all die. Your mother, grandmother and all three of you."

"We'll just have to see."

This was the time for the three of them to come together. It was time to bind their magic. Anja knew the only way for it to happen is by trusting each other. At that moment, she did.

Vincent signaled them with his eyes. At once, they united their palms together to forge their magic. They hoped it would break the witch's hold on them.

The moment the three palms came together, the earth began to quake, but this result was only temporary as the witch was more powerful. She separated their hands with loud screaming, and they all fell to the ground. Vincent and Katie were both shocked to see that Anja was more powerful than they could have ever imagined.

At that moment, the witch dropped on the ground. "Guess what? I knew how strong you were. I was ready for it."

A bright ball of light blinded them for an instant, but it was all the time Xalena needed.

"Inastua vershus!" Xalena quickly pinned Anja and Vincent down, breaking their magic. She was ready to kill them both.

"No!" Katie's lips shook as she watched them struggle. If she failed to rescue them, they would all perish. She needed to sacrifice her own vial of tears to save them.

"What am I to do with you?" The witch floated in the wind towards where Katie stood.

"I'd rather die than let you touch me."

Katie closed her eyes and conjured the darkest part of her powers. It would be the most potent magic she'd ever done. One that would come at a considerable price.

It caught the witch off guard.

"Anja!" she cried tossing the vial in her direction. "It's all up to you!"

Catching the vial, she quickly rolled and opened it. Taken in the entire contents, her wounds rapidly healed. Power radiated throughout her body. With her eyes aglow, Anja pulled the power inside her. Focusing on Xalena, she smiled.

"I have had enough of you!"

The first blow knocked the witch to the other side of the cavern. By the time Xalena was able to get her bearing, Anja was already on her. Her blows were lightning quick, never giving Xalena a chance to get in one hit.

Finally, Anja bound the witch. Holding her own blade to her throat, she was given a choice.

"Open the waters, or you can meet your end right now."

"You wouldn't dare," she sneered.

"Look into my eyes and see whether I am lying. My mother will die. My grandmother will die."

"Go ahead," Xalena laughed. "I've already sold myself. I've made my deal with the real devil!"

Pressing the knife to Xalena's throat just enough to draw blood, "I will die, whether or not my father catches up to me. Like you said earlier, 'what's one more witch?'"

It was true. Drawing on her powers, Xalena healed herself and then allowed the water to flow once again.

Katie quickly filled the vials.

"Anja," Katie called, "come drink."

As Anja turned, Xalena had one more trick up her sleeve. Knocking Anja off her feet, she opened a porthole.

"Good luck trying to save the other witches!" she spat. Spying the amulet, "I guess I'll take this as your offering after all," Xalena laughed at them she stole Anja's amulet.

As she tossed the amulet in, she laughed, "Try to receive it now!" Xalena followed right behind.

As the Well of Rites begins to shut down, Anja tried to catch the last of water flowing in her hands. She was too late. The precious liquid was gone.

"Your mother's amulet, Anja!" Vincent called out.

When the illumination had faded, Vincent realized that the great porthole had swallowed the witch and the amulet. But the three of them were still breathing.

"Damn it!" he swore. "I'm sorry Anja. Katie."

"You tried Vincent. For now, that's the most important thing."

Running his hands through his hair, "But it wasn't enough."

"One battle at a time," Anja affirmed. "One battle at a time."

Taking a deep breath, Vincent agreed. "The first thing we must do is restore your powers."

"Agreed," both sisters declared.

Vincent held out his hand towards Katie. Placing one of the vials in his hand, "we came a long way for this."

"But this is the last of the water."

"For now it is."

"Yes. Once we get you back to your full powers; we can do the same for your Régine and your mother."

Anja thought about seeing Régine. She has a lot of explaining to do. There would be so many questions Anja wanted answers to.

Anja eyed the water. It had a bit of a pungent odor, but it was to be expected.

"Here's to better health," she said as she tossed it back.

The water was cold as well as tingly as it slid down Anja's throat. Both Katie and Vincent looked at her in anticipation to see it was working.

"Should I be feeling anything?" she asked Vincent with the last drop gone.

"Give it a moment. You'll know when it's happening. You might want to sit down for it."

The suggestion came a little too late. Being thrown to her knees, Anja felt her body heaving and constricting. She could feel the surge of energy beginning at the soles of her feet and slowly making its way up.

"Will Régine go through this? Or our mother?" Katie whispered to Vincent watching Anja go through the transformation.

"I don't know the state your mother is in. As for you Régine, I was able to stabilize her and keep her from sinking more."

"With Anja's powers almost gone when she was given the tears, this is better than it could be. It will pass a lot quicker for her now."

When it seemed like the pain had begun to subside, Vincent helped her up. He could see the glow returning to her eyes. Her hands felt warm in his.

"How do you feel?"

The tingly sensation just radiated in and through her body. A smile came to her face.

"I feel like I am more than back. The energy I feel now."

"It will level out and subside a bit in time," Vincent reassured her, "but it will always be more than what you began with."

"Anja, mother's amulet is gone. We have to get it back."

"Katie, I've held onto the amulet so long. But my mother is alive. Our mother. Right now, the amulet is not important."

"Katie," Vincent began, "we'll find it. I promise."

Chapter Eleven

"So what will you do now?" Katie asked Anja.

The two sisters looked at each other. They both understood the sacrifices they both made. The sacrifices still to be made. But Anja not only has her mother, but also a younger sister. She still had to wrap her head around that.

"Save our grandmother first. Once I know she is safe, I will come to you and our mother."

Pulling Anja to his side, "we will come," Vincent added.

Vincent stood so close to Anja. It felt like coming home. For the time, in a long time, she was grateful he was there.

"Do you want to return with us? I want Régine to know it was you who helped us."

Katie shrugged her shoulders. "Do you think she will welcome me?"

A slight smile rose on Anja's face. "I'm sure of it. You're blood. To Régine, there is nothing more important."

"I will go with you. Thank you."

The sisters directly looked at one another. It was a long strained silence before Vincent slightly coughed.

Standing in front of the two women, "I don't know about you two, but this looks like a moment for a sisterly hug."

Anja and Katie both turned and looked at him with the same expression of horror.

Throwing his hands in front of him, "yeah, you two are sisters. Let's get a move on it. Long hike back down before we get to the truck."

Reaching the truck, they quickly threw their belonging in the back of the second row. Anja observed Vincent packing the sacred water with extra protection. He knew it had to get back intact being the last of the water. Perhaps, in reality, it was a chance for them. Bond or no bond, this was something she was going to consider once her grandmother was up and about again.

"Okay, ladies," Vincent announced as he slapped the hood of his truck, "time to get back to the city."

With Katie prepared to also drive, the trio made it back to the city and less than a day. With her and Vincent driving in four-hour shifts, the need to stop was far and few between. Anja was grateful Katie didn't drive as fast as Vincent.

"I know you're overwhelmed right now, I can't imagine how you feel...," Katie said to Anja. "Not only is your mother alive, but you also having a sister. On top of that, your father wants you dead. That can't give you a good feeling. It's emotional overload."

"I think I understand why she kept you hidden," Vincent said trying to spin it. "As a child, you wouldn't have reached your full potential. He would have killed you without a second thought."

Turning Anja towards him, "They thought they were doing what was for the best for you."

"But still a father who would want to kill his own child is just evil," Katie added.

"He does sound monstrous," Anja murmured. "We are the same blood...does that make me evil?"

"It's true," Vincent pointed out, "his blood is in you, and so is your mother's. You are powerful. Very powerful. Look at the feat you just accomplished."

Vincent noticed they were running low on gas as he pulled into a gas station.

"Excellent timing. You need anything? Anja? Katie?"

"No," they said in unison, laughing afterward.

As Vincent filled up the tank, Anja watched him and sighed.

"I've never really felt powerful before. Not until..." Anja looked at Vincent.

"How long have you two been together?" Katie asked.

"We think actually just started again." Anja mused, "now that we're bound, we'll see how things are."

"He really does seem like a good man. I think he really does love you." Katie moved forward, "that's the energy I'm getting."

Anja smiled, looking at Vincent again. "I believe he does."

Chapter Twelve

Maria was happy to see Anja at home. Her happiness turned to bewilderment when she saw an extra person. Anja and Katie stood side by side in Régine's living room. Maria could see their resemblance was uncanny. Looking between them, she was more than perplexed.

"I see you found a friend on the way," Maria said to Anja.

"Would you believe she's actually my sister, Katie? Katie, this is our good friend, Maria."

"Sister? Oh my goodness!" Maria pulled Katie into a hug. "This has been an eventful trip!"

"Yes, it has," Vincent added.

"I've been looking after Régine," Maria mentioned to Katie.

"Thank you," Katie said. She really didn't know what to make of Maria's lime green outfit.

"How is she doing?" Anja asked once she reached their grandmother's bedside.

"I was worried," Maria began. "I could barely feel a pulse. I wasn't sure if you would make it back in time."

"I didn't either." Anja pulled the vial from the rucksack. "Help me lift her head and neck back."

"Is this water from the well?" Maria asked.

"Yes, it is," Vincent answered.

"Thank you," Maria hugged him so quick; the air flew from his lungs.

Anja slowly poured the water so that her grandmother would not choke as it went down.

Wringing her hand, Maria whispered, "now what?"

"Now we wait," Katie said.

Anja said, looking at Vincent, "Do you think maybe it's too late?"

Walking towards Anja, "No I don't."

"How can you be so sure?" Anja asked feeling as if it was an eternity.

Motioning towards her grandmother, he said, "Take a look for yourself."

The color returned quickly to Régine's complexion. The translucent of her skin was slowing dissipating. The sisters could see she was breathing easier. Régine's eyes gradually open, glazed over with the fragments of a nightmare. Everything was fuzzy as she didn't recognize where she was for a moment.

"It worked," Anja said.

"I knew it would," Katie responded.

Régine swallowed. She licked her lips, trying to wet her mouth.

"There's a glass of water on the bedside table," Maria pointed out.

Katie took the cool glass while Anja slowly lifted Régine's head.

"Easy now, Régine," Anja murmured. "Take your time."

Régine looked at her two granddaughters. The truth she's been hiding all these years has finally surfaced. The look in Anja's eyes told her everything.

"I will answer your questions now, Anja."

"You need to rest."

"No," Régine started, "I need to get this stone off my chest."

At that point, Anja knew there was no point arguing. "Régine, this is..."

"Yes, I know — your sister. I can see your mother in her eyes just as I have with you, Anja. It was the one thing that I cherish knowing I could see my child within you."

"Why didn't you tell me?" she whispered.

"Your mother was young when she met your father. Young and in love. In her eyes, he could do no wrong. When his true colors, true nature surfaced, it was too late." Régine indicated. "Your father would never allow her to leave him, especially not with his child."

Vincent looked at Anja; he could see she was really trying to keep it together. He stood behind her. Wrapping his arms around her torso encircling her waist, he held her close.

"Azrail is the reason she faked her death. Creating the illusion your mother was never pregnant; he would never have a reason to look for you."

Régine, pause for a moment before finishing.

"Once done, we placed a powerful protection spell over not just you, but for me also."

"So that your powers would continue to protect Anja and keep her hidden," Vincent added.

"Exactly. When I realized that it was Azrail draining powers from the witches, it was too late." Looking towards Anja, "I'm sorry, my dear, it was a mistake."

"Sorry for having me believe my mother was dead all this time?" tears shimmered in her eyes. "She's my mother!"

"Shhh, it's okay" Victor whispered. Speaking clearly, "It's out in the open now."

"That was her secret to tell you, not mine. You should have never found out about your father this way."

"That means we will have to face your father. Are you ready for that?"

"I have no choice but to be ready," Anja spoke with conviction. "Enough witches have already died by my father's hand."

"You can't blame yourself, Anja," Katie reminded her.

"I know this. What I also know is I can't stand by and watch it happen."

"You know that I will be at your side," Vincent declared.

Anja turned, looking at him and smiled. "You know, I was hoping that you said that."

"Really? Why is that?"

"I kind of like having you around."

Kissing Anja's knuckles, "I kind of like being around."

Régine watched their exchange, exclaimed, "You two are bound?"

"Yes, Régine."

"Yes, ma'am," Vincent replied nodding as he pulled Anja into a deep embrace.

Anja could feel the blush creeping up her face.

"You don't know just how happy you two have just made me," Régine spoke quietly with tears welling in her eyes.

Anja hugged her grandmother. She closed her eyes and drew in a lung full of Régine's familiar smell. She craved this over the past week.

"Régine, this past week has shown me the sacrifices you've made not only to me but our mother too."

"I know you will do whatever it takes. Now, I want to speak to your sister."

"How is your mother doing?" turning her attention to Katie.

"She is also losing her power. It the reason I finally met my sister. To get the water to save her."

As Anja watched Régine and Katie have some private time, she felt the most intense feeling of relief. A huge burden lifted from her shoulders.

"Katie will take the last vial to our mother."

"You don't want to go with her?" Vincent asked.

Anja responded, "Not right away. Without the witch at the well, we will have to find another way to help the others,"

Katie had to agree. "I'll let mother know."

"Katie, you are so beautiful. I am sorry I never watch you learn to crawl and walk. Your first tooth."

Anja turned to Vincent and said, "We did it. We did it."

"I have the feeling there's not much we couldn't do together, Anja."

"I have the same feeling," she told him.

"Blood or no blood. Azrail will not win this." Anja said to the group.

Wrapping his arms around her, Vincent held her close to him.

"We will do it together."

About the Author

Renee Joiner is a writer on a mission to awaken people to their greatest potential through the power of storytelling infused with mysticism, modern paganism, and new age spirituality. At the young age of 12, she began rigorously studying the fascinating philosophy of Wicca. By the time she was 20, she was self-initiated into the craft, and hasn't looked back ever since. To this day, she has authored over 35 books pertaining to the magick and mysteries of life.

Originally from Long Island, New York, Renee is now a proud inhabitant of Northeast Florida; however, she considers herself to be a citizen of Mother Earth. When she doesn't have a book or pen in hand, she loves exploring new places and learning new things. And being the nature lover that she is, she considers herself to be an avid animal advocate.

To find out more about Renee Joiner artistically, spiritually, and personally, feel free to visit her official website at **www.mojosiedlak.com.**

www.ingramcontent.com/pod-product-compliance
Lightning Source LLC
Chambersburg PA
CBHW020355130626
46549CB00006B/2295